NOT SO HERO

By Julian Lopez

Copyright 2026
By Julian Lopez
All Rights Reserved.

No part of this book may be reproduced, stored in a retrieval system, or transmitted by any means, electronic, mechanical, photocopying, recording, or otherwise, without written permission from the publisher.

ISBN: 979-8-234-01460-3
Library of Congress Control Number: 2019905223

Published by Inkwell Books LLC
10632 North Scottsdale Road, Unit 695
Scottsdale, AZ 85254
Tel. 480-315-3781
E-mail info@inkwellbooksllc.com
Website www.inkwellbooksllc.com

CONTENTS

PROLOGUE

Deep breathes through his nose out of anger and sorrow. Javier is his name. He's a 24-year-old retired gang leader.

He's looking at a picture of his wife and daughter. The non-stop thought of their premature death.

"BANG" "BANG" "Baby! Riley!" Javier shouted, rushing to his bleeding family. He's getting flashbacks of hearing the ambulance, the ride to the hospital, and the wife's family yelling at Javier. He has one final flashback of his wife and daughter's funeral. The image of the killer's gun with the inscription "Diablo" is tattooed in his brain. He is out for blood and won't quit until he finds the killer and gets his revenge.

"Boss,Boss!" Javier comes back to reality.

"What is it, Gonzalez?" he asked as he slowly started breathing. Gonzalez is one of the group leads, along with Hudson and Ramirez alongside them. "Is this it?" Javier questioned.

"Yes this is supposedly their hideout."

"We don't know how many there are, but the four of us can do this."

"Right!" they collectively said.

CHAPTER 1:
Nothing Left

They put their hoods on and rushed through the entry of an abandoned warehouse. Bullets are firing all across the warehouse. Javier and his group members take cover behind a stack of pallets. Javier's group killed most of the men but bullets kept them from advancing. A green sphere shaped item slid across the room, next to Javier.

"Grenade!" Gonzalez ran and picked it up. He ran towards the remaining men.

"Diaz is upstairs!" exclaimed Gonzalez.

"Gonzalez!" "BOOM" the explosion echoes across the warehouse. "Damn it!" Javier yelled while running up the staircase.

They ran down the hall to the only door across from the stairs. Hudson stood by the left side, Ramirez on the right. Javier kicked in the door and then leaped back. The rival leader Diaz was in the room behind a tall and buff man.

"Rocky, if you would?" Diaz said in confidence.

"Don't interfere, he's mine," Javier said.

Javier walked toward Rocky. Rocky rushed toward Javier

and grappled him. Javier delivered a quick jab to Rocky's ribs, landing an elbow on the back of his head, then kicking the back of his knees. Rocky kneeling takes Javier's knee to the skull and is knocked unconscious. Javier stomped his head twice to be sure.

"You're next?" he said to Diaz as he caught his breath.

"BANG" "BANG" followed by two thuds on the ground. Javier turned around to see Ramirez and Hudson's limp bodies on the ground. He looked up to see Gonzalez aiming his gun at him.

"I'm pretty sure you're next," Gonzalez said grinning.

Javier's eyes widened seeing the gun. Gonzalez shows the inscription "Diablo."

"Look familiar Javi?"

"Y–you killed?"

"Your wife and that brat? Guilty," Gonzalez chuckled. Javier grits his teeth, shaking out of anger. "I'll kill you!" he yelled and took a step. Gonzalez shoots by Javier's feet.

"Don't move, I won't hesitate."

"I have nothing left. Do it," Javier sighed.

"Just like that? What happened to the 'Unstoppable Leader'?"

Javier just stood silently and glared at Gonzalez. He feels a burning sensation behind his left shoulder. "Agh!" Javier yelled in pain. Diaz stabbed him. Javier fell into a kneeling position facing Diaz.

"Don't worry, you'll meet your family soon," Diaz said.

Javier put his hand on the shoulder with the knife and

yanked it out while sprinting past Diaz and slashing his thigh. Diaz yelled in pain while Javier held the knife up to his throat from behind.

"You're starting to piss me off," Javier said, glaring at Gonzalez.

"Javi, you can't win this."

"If this is it for me, I'm taking you both with me."

Javier pushes Diaz towards Gonzalez, forcing him to shoot Diaz accidentally. Javier rushed Gonzalez, knocking the gun out of his hand. Javier sliced Gonzalez's hand and across his chest. He kicked him against the wall.

"Tough bastard aren't you?" Gonzalez chuckled as he spat blood out.

Javier went for another kick but Gonzalez blocked it and punched Javier in the face. Back and forward trading punches. Javier punched Gonzalez's chest wound, grabbed his face and slammed his head against the wall.

"I treated you like family!" Javier said in sorrow.

"Then I'll take us both out like your family," Gonzalez then bear-hugged Javier. Diaz pulled out a grenade, pulled the pin and threw it. Javier sees it, pulls out his gun, and proceeds to shoot Gonzalez to let go.

"BANG" "BANG" "BANG"

Javier ran towards the door, "Too late Rios," Diaz said.

"BOOM"

Javier slowly opens his eyes and sees nothing but a cloud he's on as if in the sky.

"Hello, chosen hero!" said a woman.

Javier pointed his gun at her, surprised; she looked shocked.

"Where am I? Who are you?" the lady calmly walks closer to Javier.

"Young Hero, My name is Aisha. I am the goddess of another world."

"BANG"

"I'm not in the mood for jokes. I don't know what this is but I'm leaving," Javier said.

"H-Hey, can you please hear me out first? It's not a joke," she said, startled. She continued. "I'm here to give you a second chance at life."

"OK, I'm done, where's the exit?"

"There is no exit hero."

"Why do you keep calling me that? I'm not who you're looking for. My name is Javier."

"Javier, I'm sending you to a new world."

"What are you talking about? I don't need this. I'm going home."

"But Hero, you're dead."

Javier stood there with a look of confusion and shock. He was only able to let out one word.

"Huh?"

CHAPTER 2:

A Hero Was Made

"What do you mean I'm dead?" Javier said in disbelief.

"That explosion you tried to escape, you were too late."

Javier puts his hands on his head. He can't believe it.

"God damn it!" Javier yells as he tries collecting his thoughts.

"Calm down Hero," Aisha said.

Javier grits his teeth.

"So what now? Do I descend to hell or something?"

"No, as I said before, I'm giving you a second chance at life."

"Meaning?"

Aisha flicks her hair back and clears her throat.

"Hello Javier, you have been chosen to be the hero of this world. I am Aisha, the goddess of this world. I saw how you suffered in your past life. I want to grant you a wish."

"A wish?"

"Yes, anything you could possibly want."

"Even for a peaceful life with my wife and daughter?"

"If that is what you desire."

"Yes, that's my wish!" Javier yelled in temptation.

"Before I grant your wish, I have a task for you."

"I knew it!"

"Correct. You have been chosen to be the hero of this world to defeat the Demon Lord and to protect the world's peace."

"So all I have to do is take out some guy named 'Demon Lord' and I'll get my wish?"

"Not exactly. His name is Kaval. He is an actual demon and the ruler of the Demon Kingdom."

"Hold up! You want me to fight an actual demon?"

"Correct."

"No!" Javier said in disagreement.

"What about your wish?"

"What makes you think I'd possibly win? It's a demon."

"You'd be granted powers."

"Powers?"

"In this world, magic exists. Monsters and other races unfamiliar in your past world exist."

"Uh huh, So why do I have to do this?"

"To restore peace in the world."

"It's not even my world! You said you're the goddess, why can't you handle it?"

"It's not how it works. We aren't allowed to interfere with these worlds, we only watch over them."

"So you're making it my problem?"

Aisha claps and the sound silences Javier unwillingly.

"I have chosen you to be the hero of this world. I see potential in you to defeat the Demon Lord. I'll grant you hero powers and allow you to take your personal belongings on your person."

"My knife and my gun? I'm pretty sure it'll take more than that and fireballs to beat a demon, let alone a Demon Lord."

"The Hero's power levels up your weapons and you can use all elements of magic including but not limited to fire, water, earth, air, darkness, and the hero's specialty; light."

"Light? What will that do? I blind him and I get a cheap shot in?"

"Light magic is the same as holy magic. It deals more damage to demons."

Javier grins in satisfaction.

"Your gun, however, will be modified," Aisha explains.

"You can reload using earth magic because guns do not exist in this world. It will also have a healing ability."

Javier hesitates a little but is determined to reclaim his family.

"Alright, I'll do it. With all these powers, I can kick the demon lord's ass," Javier says in confidence.

"One last thing, great hero. You will meet warriors you'll take with you to team up against the demon army."

"Army?"

"It isn't going to be that simple. The Demon Lord is planning to attack the neighboring nations. Defeating his army is a key component to defeating the Demon Lord," Aisha explained.

"You clearly saw what happens when I work in a group!"

"You made a simple mistake."

"They took EVERYTHING!" Javier is fighting to hide his

sorrow. Aisha lands and walks up to Javier. She grabs his hands. He looks up at her.

"Javier, I understand. If you defeat the Demon Lord and protect the world, you can live in peace with your family again. Trusting is difficult but it goes both ways. You don't have to fight alone."

Javier sucks his teeth. "Fine but let me be clear, the moment I think they're going to betray me; I won't hesitate this time," Javier warns Aisha.

"Not everyone is out to get you, young hero."

"Can you stop calling me that?"

"It's protocol, just let me do my job."

Javier sighs. "Whatever, what now?"

Aisha faces her palms towards Javier.

"Young Hero, I bestow upon you the powers of the Great Hero. You shall defeat the Demon Lord and protect the peace of this world. In exchange, you will be granted a wish of your desire. Do you accept?"

"Yeah, sure."

Aisha sighs and then grins.

"See you soon, Hero."

"What do you mean?"

A white flash filled the room. Javier opens his eyes and is in a forest with a trail beside him.

Javier pulls out a photo of his family. Javier sighs.

"This is crazy. That damn goddess better keep her word."

CHAPTER 3:
The New World

"So this is the new world? Doesn't seem that much different," Javier thought as he looked around.

A carriage is approaching, causing him to be on guard.

The carriage stopped right next to Javier.

"Hello, what are you doing out here?" the driver asked.

"I just got here."

"Where are you from?"

"Someplace far away."

"Well I'm heading towards the next town over. Would you like a ride?"

"Really?" Javier felt suspicious about the driver.

A sudden noise of rustling from the bushes caught their attention. Javier quickly turned towards the bushes, gun in hand, aiming in that direction. A Bear jumped out and roared at Javier.

"Oh shit!" Javier yelled. He jumped back and shot at the bear.

"BANG" "BANG"

The bear visibly hurt rushed Javier and knocked the gun

out of Javier's hand. He held his hands out, grappling the bear's wrists.

"If you want to survive then get the hell out of here!" Javier yelled to the driver.

The driver got off his carriage and pulled out a staff.

"What are you doing?" Javier yelled.

"Stone Bullet!" the driver chanted.

A small rock appeared and was flying towards the bear. It scratched the bear's arms, catching its attention. Javier pulled the bear close and kneed it in the stomach, launching the bear into a tree and snapping the tree off its stem.

"HUH?" said both the driver and Javier.

Javier was taken aback and looked at his hands. Out of curiosity he punched a tree, breaking off a big chunk of the tree. The driver again is in shock. Javier grins.

"Sir, who are you exactly?" asked the driver.

"Javier. I'm going after the Demon Lord."

"What? T-T-The Demon Lord?"

"Right. It's a long story I don't have the time to explain. If you were serious about giving me a ride, I'll take you up on that deal."

"What about the bear?"

Javier looked at the limp bear carcass.

"What about it?" Javier asked while picking up his gun.

"I don't have room for it in my carriage."

"Why would we take it?"

"You can sell hunted animals."

"How much would it go for?"

"A bear this size is a bit difficult to hunt; I'd say it would be quite the handsome amount."

Javier grabbed a rope from the carriage.

"Mind if I borrow this?" Javier asked as he walked towards the bear.

"Not at all. What for?"

Javier drags the bear towards the carriage by its foot. He tied a knot around its ankle and another to the carriage. Javier hops on the carriage next to the driver.

"I don't know if..."

"Let's go."

"But the bear."

"Let's go," Javier insisted.

The driver signaled his horse to go. The bear is being dragged across the ground.

"You're quite the unique individual," the driver said.

"I've been told."

"May I ask? Why are you aiming for the Demon Lord?"

"I'd rather not get into it. It's a long story."

"I see. You have your reasons."

"Would you like to go with me?"

"W-What? Are you insane?"

"One could say, but I don't have anything to lose and defeating the Demon Lord would benefit me."

"Why do something so dangerous?"

"Isn't the Demon Kingdom planning to attack?"

"The demons haven't caused any trouble for over 100 years ever since the previous Hero defeated the past corrupt Demon Lord."

"I heard they're planning to attack in the future."

"Where did you hear that?"

"A goddess mentioned it to me."

The carriage stopped violently. The driver looked Javier in the eyes.

"Are you the descendant of the hero?" the driver asked.

"A what?"

"You must be the chosen one! If what you're saying is true, you must be the hero to save us from the current Demon Lord!"

Javier sat silently in confusion about how he jumped to that conclusion.

"Your strength is above the human average. You also possess that strange weapon," he says, pointing at Javier's gun.

"My gun?"

"Gun?"

"Yeah, it shoots bullets at what I aim at and it apparently can heal too."

"That is quite a unique device."

"Really? It's common where I'm from."

The driver sits back astonished. The carriage begins moving again. After some time they reach the entrance of the town's gate. The first guard checks the driver's ID.

"Can I see your ID?" asks the second guard.

Javier looks confused.

"Your ID? I can't allow you in without one."

Javier pulls out his wallet and hands over his ID to the guard. The guard is confused looking at Javier's ID from his past world.

"I've never seen one like this. Is he with you?" the guard asked the driver.

"He's a new assistant," the driver said enthusiastically.

Javier bit his tongue and looked blankly at the guards, nodding in agreement.

The guards look at each other and then step aside. The carriage passes through. The bear is dragged along through the gate. The guards look at the bear in confusion. The driver and Javier take the bear to a merchant. They sold the bear for four gold and three silver coins. Javier looks at it.

"How much is this?" Javier asks.

"That is 275 Marbs."

Javier looks confused.

"Marbs is our currency. Copper coins are worth 10, silver are worth 25, gold is worth 50, and platinum is 100. You would have received much more if you sold it at the guild," the driver explains.

"Then why didn't we?"

"You need to be an adventurer and have an adventure license."

"Where would I go to get one?"

The driver leads Javier to the guild. Javier stands in front of the guild. He turns around.

"That reminds me. I never got your..." the driver is gone.

"Name? Oh ok then," Javier said in confusion.

Javier is about to enter the guild but suddenly gets a flashback of when he would enter the abandoned warehouse back in his past world. He returns to reality and puts on his hood as he enters the guild. Everybody stops what they're doing and looks at Javier. He sighs knowing it's going to be pain.

"That damn goddess," he mumbled under his breath.

Javier starts walking towards the front desk and everyone looks at him. The driver is walking along a mountainside path. He enters a palace and is in front of a man with long white hair and crimson red eyes.

"I've come with very important information," the driver said.

The white haired man stares at the driver and signals him to continue with his hands.

"It seems The Hero has returned and is informed of your plans. He doesn't seem familiar with this world; however, he seems to be powerful."

"I see. Well done, you may leave," the white haired man said in a deep voice.

The driver bows and walks away.

"So the hero returns? Things are going to get interesting," the man says and laughs evilly.

CHAPTER 4:

The Hero Is Here

Javier approaches the desk.

"Hello, welcome to the adventurers guild," said the receptionist.

The receptionist's name is Elly. She is a beautiful elf with long blonde hair. She has a personality that has all the men wanting to work under a contract with her.

"Yeah, I need an adventuring license," Javier said with a blank face.

He hears other adventurers talking about him.

"Newbie thinks he's ready for the big leagues?"

"How dare he talk so casually with Elly?"

"I bet he's hiding his ugly face under that hood."

Javier ignores them and continues. Elly handed him a form to fill out.

"Fill this out to get you started," she says smiling.

Javier starts writing. The guild begins to get quiet. A big man in gold armor approaches Javier along with two more large men.

"It's him, the town's number one adventurer," an adventurer whispered.

"Hey newbie, move it! I got business to deal with," says the man in gold armor.

Javier continues writing. The armored man gets irritated for being ignored.

"Hey I'm talking to you!" he yells at Javier.

Javier stops writing and glares at the armored man without turning his head. The three men were taken aback. The adventurer has had enough, so he yanks Javier's hood down. Suddenly, his chest plate is in Javier's left hand and his right hand holding his knife up to the armored man's throat. They are face-to-face.

"I'm only going to say this once so shut up and listen. Touch or bother me again; I'll put you in the ground. The same goes for your sidekicks," Javier said, irritated.

He aggressively releases the man's chest plate and puts away his knife. Javier continues with filling out the form.

"I'm the number one adventurer of this town! Some commoner trash will not threaten me!" the adventurer yells.

He darts at Javier ready to throw a punch. Javier dodges underneath the punch, grabs the adventurer's wrist, and slams him into the ground. The adventure is halfway on the floor-board's unconscious. Javier then looks at his two comrades furiously. The two comrades ran out of the guild in fear. The entire guild is in shock.

"No way he just beat Rex with a single bodyslam!" an adventurer said in disbelief.

Javier turns back to the form and hands it to Elly.

"Alright, let me just review this and..." She stops reading and looks at Javier.

"Is everything alright?" Javier asked.

"Javier, it's not good to lie on your form," she said with concern.

"I'm not."

"One moment please," Elly said as she took the form to the back room. Minutes go by. Adventures continues talking about Javier.

"He doesn't look like it but seems really strong."

"Should we recruit him into our party?"

"He seems dangerous."

Javier is getting annoyed listening to strangers talk about him.

"Hey!" Javier yells.

The guild went silent. All the attention is on Javier.

"I don't care about your opinions, but I don't like it if you have something to say and you won't say it to my face! So if you have something to say, I'm right here!"

The guild stays quiet. Elly and an older gentleman come out.

"Are you the new guy who put his rank down as Hero?" asked the old man pointing at Javier.

"HUH?" the guild expressed.

"Yeah, and?" Javier responded.

"It's not allowed to lie on your form. From the lack of experience, there is no way you're Hero Rank."

"I wasn't sure what it meant by Rank. I'm the Hero,"

The old man's eyes widened and he rushed up to Javier. He grabs Javier's wrists and pulls him to the back room. Elly, Javier, and the old man sit across from each other.

"What do you mean you're the hero?" the old man asked.

"I'm the Hero of this world who has to defeat the Demon Lord who is planning to start a war."

"That's impossible! We have a 'Cease Fire' contract with the Demon Kingdom."

"Look, the goddess told me that the Demon Lord is ready to fire again."

"Goddess?" the old man rushes to his file cabinet, pulling out a file titled "Hero."

"The Hero was informed by a goddess that the Demon lord was attempting to conquer the neighboring countries to gain power. The Hero defeated the Demon Lord and lost his life in the process," the old man read.

Elly looks at Javier in complete shock.

"Alright, when will he attack?" asked the old man.

"I don't know. All I know is he is building his army. I was left with the mission of getting stronger, forming a party, and defeating the Demon Lord. I'm guessing there is still time to prepare."

"In that case, I'll give you an adventuring license and start you off as a C Rank."

"Sure but who the hell are you exactly to call the shots?"

"He is the guild master," Elly explained.

Javier is not impressed.

"Right. Anyway, I need to get stronger so I'll take a quest now," Javier said.

"Well, since it's your first quest maybe you can start with an F Rank quest?" Elly suggested.

"No, I need something more challenging. I have time but not enough time to help old people cross the road. I need to fight monsters or something useful," Javier said in a stern voice.

Elly looks at Javier and looks upset.

"Dammit," Javier sighed.

Javier walks up to Elly and kneels. He puts his hand on her shoulder. Elly is shocked. Javier sighs deeply.

"Listen, I'm sorry. Everything is happening so fast and it's a lot to take in all at once," Javier said gently.

Elly turns slightly red. "I-It's ok. We're here to support you."

Javier gets up and sits back down.

"I should let you know that I won't trust you guys so easily."

"If I may suggest, I believe you'd find more challenging quests in the Royal Capital," said the guild leader.

"A town full of entitled rich kids? Sounds like a great idea!" Javier said sarcastically.

"Not everyone is bad and besides, this is a national emergency. Some of the nation's best fighters and adventurers are located there. We'll also put word out throughout the entire nation that The Hero is looking for the best of the best to help defeat the Demon Lord," the guild leader said.

Javier sighs. "Fine, old man, I'll recruit there then."

"I'll pretend you didn't say the first part. It's settled then; I'll assign you a carriage. It'll be about a 3-day trip. Both you and Elly will go."

"WHAT?" both Javier and Elly are shocked.

"Elly, I'm transferring you to the Royal Capital Guild. I need someone there the Hero can trust," said the guild leader.

"What part of 'not trusting easily' didn't you get?"

"It'll be fine. Elly, I'm trusting you."

"R-Right," Elly says unsure.

They complete Javier's adventures license and are now off to the Royal Capital.

CHAPTER 5:
To the Royal Capital

Within the first hour, neither Javier nor Elly has said a word.

"Do I make you nervous?" Javier asked.

"What? It's not that."

"Look, you didn't have to come along with me. You could've just said, 'No'."

"No, I was trusted with this assignment."

"You haven't said anything for the past hour. You uncomfortable or something?"

"Well, aren't you? You haven't said anything either. You seem like you don't want me here."

"Well you're not wrong."

Elly sighs.

"But I appreciate that you did. We're stuck together until this ends. Plus, I don't dislike you so far," Javier explained.

"But you don't trust me?"

"Did anyone hear me when I said that I didn't? Look, you seem sweet but I don't trust that the most."

"Well what if we got to know each other? We could build

trust off of that."

"I don't know," Javier hesitates.

"You said it yourself, we're stuck together so why not get along?"

"Look, i-it's hard."

"Why?"

Javier looks away. Elly puts her hand on Javier's shoulder. Javier has his hand on his gun. He looks at her. She is smiling.

"It's okay," she says.

Javier looks at Elly for a few seconds.

"Fine, I'll tell you. This stays between us," Javier explained.

Javier explained everything that had happened to his wife and daughter being murdered, his life before quitting the gang, and how he got to the new world. Elly was understanding to the best of her abilities. They go back and forth as they talk and learn new things about each other. The carriage eventually stops once it gets dark. They set up camp, made a fire, and had dinner.

"So Hero, what about now?" Elly asks.

"What do you mean?"

"Do you trust me now?"

"I trust you enough not to kill me in my sleep."

There is an awkward pause. Javier chuckles,

"I'm kidding. I don't fully trust you but, I think I eventually can," Javier says.

"I'm glad. You should probably get some rest. You had an eventful day."

"At some point I'll rest."

"Well, don't stay up too late. Good night, Hero," Elly said, yawning.

"Javi," Javier said.

"What?"

"You don't have to call me Hero. You can call me Javi."

Elly smiles "Right, good night Javi."

"Night."

They each get in their sleeping areas. Javier lays down. He pulls out the photo of his wife and daughter, which he carries in his wallet and stares at it. He eventually falls asleep. Javier opens his eyes and is in a familiar setting.

"Hello, Hero."

"Goddess?" Javier said surprised.

"I see your first day was quite eventful."

"Damn it! Am I dead again?"

"No. While you're in a state of unconsciousness, we can communicate when we need to. As I mentioned before, I can't physically interfere but we can still communicate."

"Okay. What?"

"How come you're so rude to me? You were nice to that elf girl but not me? The loveable, cute, beautiful, smart goddess guiding you through the entire mission?" Aisha fake cries.

Javier looks at Aisha with a blank face. Aisha peeks and sees he isn't reacting much. She stops fake crying and clears her throat.

"Moving on. I see you're moving along the right path on your journey."

"There's a right path?"

"Not necessarily. I wasn't sure how quickly you'd move. I was going to suggest the Royal Capital."

"Oh no. Are you saying the 'lovable,' 'cute,' 'beautiful,' 'smart' goddess doesn't have useful information?" Javier says sarcastically.

"Of course, I do, but I don't appreciate your attitude."

Javier sighed "Fine, I'm sorry I disrespected the all-so-mighty beauty you are," he said unenthusiastically.

"Much better."

"Anyways, I need tough quests and strong allies to beat the Demon Lord, to get the hell out."

'It will still be a while. At least a year, to be exact."

"A year? You can't be serious."

"Hero, war takes time to prepare."

Javier is disappointed.

"You need to get stronger and find allies you can trust that are as strong as well," Aisha explains.

"You're right. This is going to be a pain in the ass."

"Perhaps. I will say this: I chose you because you seem capable."

"I'm in it for my wish and my family."

"That all depends on if you can defeat the Demon Lord."

"I can. I will!"

"I have one more thing to add. I see you've been using your weapons and fought hand to hand. You need to learn how to use magic."

"I've been doing fine without it."

"'Fine' won't fare well against a Demon Lord out to destroy and conquer. You can't expect to do it without skill or knowledge of magic. I'm sure you're running low on bullets as well."

Javier sighs "Fine, I'll learn magic."

"Great! With that said, until we meet again Hero. Time to wake up."

"You're not going to tell me how to learn magic?"

Aisha disappears. Javier regains consciousness. He is the only one awake. He stands up and walks toward the carriage. A growl in the forest caught his attention. He gets a flashback.

"You need to learn how to use magic," Aisha said.

A pack of wolves jumped out from the forest. The carriage driver and Elly wake up abruptly. They run towards the carriage in fear. Javier pulls out his gun.

"You need to learn how to use magic," he hears in his head.

"I get it!" Javier yells while putting away his gun.

He stands there thinking. He gets another flashback from when he first arrived in the new world.

He puts his hands forward and chants, "Stone Bullet!" A big rock shoots out of his hands, hitting the wolf in the pack's center. He looks at his hands and grins.

"Stone Bullet!" "Stone Bullet!" "Stone Bullet!"

One by one, the wolves go down.

"Well then. Not too bad if I do say so myself."Javier says.

Both the driver and Elly look at the wolf carcasses.

"Let's go. "Javier says.

"What about the equipment?" the driver asks.

Javier looks at the equipment.

He places his palm to his face. "This is going to be a long three days."

They cleaned up the camp and loaded up the carriage.

"Wait, do you have rope? Maybe a few sacks?" Javier asks the driver.

The carriage starts moving with five wolves in a sack tied up being dragged along.

"Are you sure this is a good idea?" Elly asks.

"Don't worry, I did this with a bear before," Javier says.

"A bear?"

Days pass and the carriage finally reaches the Royal Capital.

"ID please," the first guard says as he sees five wolves tied to the carriage.

Elly hands over her ID, which looks like Javier's.

"You were an adventurer?" Javier asks.

The carriage enters the gate.

"Yes, that was years ago when I was a teenager. That's in the past now," Elly says with an embarrassed tone.

Elly hands a scroll to the guard and says "We need to speak with the King. It's urgent."

"You can have the wolves," Javier said to the driver who was not pleased with it.

They are escorted to the King's Castle. They enter a doorway to be welcomed to a public hearing. Javier looks around.

"I have a horrible feeling about this," Javier says.

CHAPTER 6:
The King and the Hero

A man walks out holding a scroll.

"Thank you all for attending today's hearing. Let's now welcome his majesty, King Axel Hiddleston the Third!" the man says.

The King comes out and sits on his throne. Everyone but Javier kneels.

"Javi, you need to kneel," Elly whispered.

"I want to try something," Javier whispered back.

"Excuse me! You're in the presence of the King!" the man says.

"I'm aware," Javier responded.

"You kneel when he enters!"

"And you are?" Javier asks in a sarcastic tone.

"My name is Harry. The King's right hand."

"Enough!" the King says.

"How dare some commoner disrespect royalty?" the King asked, annoyed.

"Royalty doesn't mean anything to me."

Everyone gasps and whispers to each other. Everyone stands back up.

"I am the one with power. Your opinion does not matter here!" the King says.

"Okay, King Hassle, my bad," Javier said sarcastically.

"Axel!"

"Not the point."

"Why are you here? We will not accept mockery of his majesty and disrespect of the kingdom!" Harry says.

Elly hands over the scroll that explains everything about Javier being the Hero and The Demon Lord preparing to attack. The King is shocked by the news.

"You're the Hero?" King Axel asked.

The entire room gasps. Javier grins.

"The Hero?"

"No way, him?"

"That's our savior?"

Javier takes two steps forward. "Yup," he says.

"I shall hear you out then," the King says annoyed.

"Alright! My name is Javier, I'm the Hero. No need to kneel to me, status isn't much to me. In about a year or so the Demon Lord is going to attack. I came to the Royal Capital to recruit for my party. I want to hold an event where I can see the best you can offer. I will pick from there. Also one last thing, this elf here is Elly and she is my receptionist at the guild. If anyone gives her a hard time," Javier pulls out his gun and knife, "you'll have to deal with me," Javier says.

Everyone is quiet and shocked about how he presented himself.

"Tough crowd," Javier said.

Afterwards, Elly and Javier left the castle.

"Javi, what was that?" Elly asked.

"I was testing his spine."

Elly looks confused.

"I was disrespecting him to test his patience and being a jerk to see how he handles it," Javier said.

"Why?"

"He is in charge here. I prefer someone with a spine. He also pisses me off with the whole 'I'm royalty' attitude."

"Javi, it would be better if you were to show some respect. Royalty aside, he still rules the country and does what he can for it."

"I get it, but I'm not changing how I do things. I was sent to protect the peace, so they better not cross me."

Elly sighs.

"Fine. I'm helping Harry make arrangements for the event, without you," Elly says.

"What? Why?"

"You need to train, we're getting you quests lined up."

They go to the guild. They approach the front desk.

"Hello, How can I help you?" asks the receptionist.

"My name is Elly. I'm a transfer receptionist. I was sent here to help him," Elly points at Javier.

"Him specifically?"

"Yes well," Elly whispers in her ear.

"The Hero?"

"That would be me," Javier says, raising his hand.

"My, Hello, Hero. I'm Lila. Feel free to come to me for anything you have questions about," says the receptionist.

"Nice try, Elly is my receptionist," Javier says playfully.

An adventurer runs up to the desk, staring at Elly.

"Are you a new receptionist? I'd like to sign with y..."

Javier kicks him aside.

"What's your problem?" said the adventurer as Javier rushes towards him.

Javier is in his face.

"Have something to say to me?" Javier threatens as he glares at the adventurer.

The adventurer gulped, "N-No, my mistake," he runs off.

"My, having a strong man to protect you must be nice," Lila teases.

"Wh-What? It's not," Elly says.

"Well, yeah," Javier interrupts.

Elly blushes.

"Anyways, I need a quest, preferably something with monsters," he hands over his license.

"Hmm, how about Stone Lizards? There was a group of them spotted near the mines," Lila suggested.

"Sure. Elly?"

"Sounds good. As I work with Harry, Lila will be your temporary receptionist," Elly said.

Lila bows to Javier.

"You'll be in my care, Great Hero."

"Right," Javier said awkwardly.

There was a brief silence between them as they looked at each other.

"Alright, well, time to get to work Javi," Elly says in a rush.

"Okay, I'm off. I'll see you tonight Elly," Javier says as he runs out with excitement.

Javier completed the mission rather quickly. He was going mission after mission as the event was nearing to begin. Javier has made a name for himself at the guild without everyone knowing he is the Hero. A week later, the time for the event arrived. Javier was sleeping in his dorm at the guild. Elly calls for him to wake him up.

"Wake up Javi."

Javier didn't wake up. Elly walks up to the side of his bed and slowly reaches for him. Javier's eyes open abruptly and he grabs Elly's wrist. He suddenly stops when he realizes it is Elly.

"My bad," he says in embarrassment.

"It's okay. Come on, we have to be at the training field soon."

"What was that about?" Elly thought.

They get to the field and sit at the judging table. Many people surround the field as participants and viewers.

"What's with the tall stage?" Javier points out.

"It's for the King," Elly explains.

"Oh great. Living large and in charge is coming to try to assert dominance," he says, annoyed.

"He's only here to watch."

"I'm well aware. I'm picking who gets a pass."

The King and Harry show up and take their seats.

"Ladies and gentlemen, we will begin the Hero party forming event!" Harry announces.

"'Hero party forming event'? That's so lame," Javier whispers.

"That wasn't the name but he was not letting you as he said 'Outshining the King'," Elly whispered.

Javier looks at Elly with disappointment.

"But before that, a few words of encouragement from the King!"

Javier rolls his eyes.

"So much for only watching," Javier thought as he rolled his eyes.

CHAPTER 7:
Forming the Hero's Party

The King stands and everyone besides Javier once again kneels. Harry and the King look at Javier bitterly. The King clears his throat.

"I'd like to commend you for coming to support your country and to help defend us from the Demon Kingdom. We thank you for your bravery and courage in taking on a very important mission. Best of luck to all of you."

Cheers and applause roar across the field.

"Now, some words from the hero," Harry said unenthusiastically.

Javier stands up and jumps on top of the King's stage. He looks at Harry and rolls his eyes. The crowd claps and cheers anticipating the Hero in the flesh. Javier clears his throat and spits off the stage. People are getting confused about how Javier is acting.

"Alright! Thank you King Hassle and little yes man!" Javier said.

Gasps spread across the field. Harry and the King are irritated.

"Yes I am the Hero, and I've been sent to defeat the Demon

Lord. I want to make this clear: I don't care about status, background, or what you think of me at any moment. I only care if you can fight and you can actually do what you're supposed to. Let's see what you got!"

Awkward applause surrounds the field as Javier returns to his seat.

"Right, there will be healers on standby in case of serious injuries. Each match will end in knock out, forfeit, or disqualification conditions. With that said, let the battles begin!" Harry announces.

"Tough crowd out there," Javier whispers to Elly.

Elly sighed knowing it would be like this. A few matches go by, Javier is not impressed or pleased with the performances so far.

"Next up, we have Gile vs Rex!" Harry announced.

Javier spat out the water he was drinking.

"What? He's here?" Javier asked, shocked.

"He was our number one adventurer in our town," Elly explained.

"I'm going to crush you!" Rex yells.

"What an idiot. That other guy though, Gile? He's got a good physique and carries a giant axe," Javier says.

Elly pulls out his file.

"He's a C Rank adventurer, same as you," Elly said.

Javier was slightly offended by that.

"His reason for joining is... finding a wife?" Elly read confused.

Javier gives her a blank stare.

"He has a special ability called 'Stomp'."

"Special ability?"

"Yes, most skilled fighters have a special ability which is a skill they gain whether with magic or physical features."

"So his 'stomp' is literal?" he asks in disappointment.

"Begin!" Harry yells.

Rex runs towards Gile at a full sprint. Gile stomps the ground and cracks the ground. The crack expands towards Rex and as soon as the crack is beneath Rex, the ground swiftly rises, launching Rex into the air. Everyone looks up in shock. Javier is amazed. As Rex falls from high up, Gile swings his axe and knocks him out of the ring.

"And the winner by knockout, Gile!"

The crowd's cheers erupted as Gile raised his axe in victory.

"Finally, we're getting somewhere," Javier says.

"Next we have Leo vs Lance!" Harry announced.

The audience was highly anticipating the match

"Lance, the King's son?"

"Leo, the failed noble?"

"This could go either way."

Elly goes through both of their files.

"Lance is the King's son, next in line for the throne. His special skill is enhanced agility. An A-Rank level skill set who is destined to be 'The King who defeated the Demon Lord'."

Javier isn't surprised. He places his palm on his forehead.

"And the other guy?"

"Leo, a member of the Vaughn family. They're considered one of the most well known noble families. Joined to gain honor and uphold the great name of the Vaughn Family," Elly read.

"Great, entitled rich kids swinging their shiny and expensive sticks," Javier said sarcastically.

"He's an A-Rank adventurer as well. He's the second son of three. He's labeled 'The failed Noble' and his special ability is called 'Switch'," Elly read.

"Failed Noble?"

"Begin!" Harry yells.

Lance lunges towards Leo. Leo blocks all of Lance's swings. Leo jumps back and chants "Switch!" His blade changes shape and length. Lance was taken aback and put his blade up to defend. "Switch!" Leo chants again as the blade switches into a jagged one. Lance's sword gets stuck between the ridges and Leo twists his blade, causing Lance to disarm. "Switch!" Leo chants holding a blade with lightning generated from the blade in front of Lance's face.

"I admit defeat," Lance says.

Leo puts away his sword and repositions his glasses as he grins.

The crowd cheers. The King is outraged. Javier sits in his thoughts and starts writing things down. The end of the event was nearing with one final match. Javier is tired and unsure who to pick for the rest of the performances. He dozes off. Elly shakes him awake.

"We're now at the final match! Maya vs Luther!" Harry announces.

Elly goes through their files. "This seems unbalanced. Maya

is a mage and Luther is a hammer wielder."

"Let's see how they deal with it," Javier says.

"Maya is nicknamed 'The Seductive Witch'."

Javier looks confused.

"She has the ability to multi-cast. And has a sharpened wand," Elly reads.

"Why a wand that's sharpened?"

Elly nods in confusion. "Her reason for joining is unknown," she reads.

"Begin!"

Maya tosses her hat to the side.

"Sorry sweetheart, looks like i got to take you down. Maybe later I can cheer you up by taking you out, for dinner that is," Luther says.

Maya sweetly smiles. "Oh my, aren't you quite the charmer?" she says as she slowly removes her robe. "You seem very manly. I don't know how I could possibly win."

Luther blushes,"W-W-Well y-you know..."

Javier is paying close attention.

Maya touches the tip of her wand "shall we?"

"I see what you mean, but her outfit doesn't portray a wizard, witch thing," Javier says confused.

"It's mage but I must agree about the outfit," Elly said.

Maya throws her wand and it punctures Luther in his shoulder. Luther let out a groan of pain. Maya rushes him and throws four quick jabs to his face. She grapples his arms and slams him onto his back. She steps on his arm holding her palm in his face with poisonous gas forming.

"So, who's taking who down?" Maya asks.

She hovers over his crotch with her right palm forming flames.

"I suggest quitting before it gets increasingly painful," Maya suggests.

"I submit!" Luther yells.

Maya pulls her wand out of Luther's shoulder and puts on her hat and robe.

"I appreciate the offer but unfortunately, I'm not interested," she says to Luther.

The crowd cheers. The men are cheering louder than any match before.

Elly in utter shock, "She's quite the character."

Javier grins and writes more notes down. Some time goes by and Harry stands as Elly hands him the list of names.

"It's time to reveal those joining the Hero on the mission to take on the Demon lord and protect our peace!" Harry announces.

"Gile Rockman!" the crowd cheers.

"Leo Vaughn!" the crowd cheers.

"And lastly, Maya Lynn!" the men cheer chaotically.

They line up in front of the King. The King stands and the three kneel.

"Congratulations, you have been bestowed the honor of teaming up to defeat the Demon Lord and keep the peace in our country and the world!" the King said.

"Yes sir!" the three yelled.

The crowd cheered and applauded for the chosen. Javier walks up to them while applauding. He suddenly stops and stares at all three of them.

“Congrats! So here’s the thing, we initiate someone in my group by circling them and then jump them, but instead, I’ll throw each of you a punch. You can block if you like,” Javier says.

The three look at each other in confusion.

“You can’t be serious, right?” Gile asks.

Javier rushes him and lands a punch to his chest, launching Gile many meters away.

“Nothing personal!” Javier yells to Gile.

Javier then walks up to Leo. Leo pulls out his sword.

“You must be insane if you think I’ll allow you to hit me. You’re no Hero,” Leo says in disgust and irritation.

“Big talk from the ‘Failed Noble’.”

Leo’s eyes widened. Javier punched Leo in the gut as he held his back with the other hand, having him kneel.

“It isn’t personal, just initiation,” Javier said.

He walks up to Maya. Maya looks at both Gile and Leo. She puts her hand on Javier’s chest.

“Hitting a woman like that wouldn’t be very heroic. How about we get out of here and go someplace, a little more private,” she whispers seductively in Javier’s ear.

Javier smiles at her and leans towards her ear.

“You’re right, that isn’t very Hero-like.”

Maya sighs in relief.

"So I'll hold back a little," he whispered.

"Huh?" Maya then crosses her arms to block.

Javier punches her arms, launching her into Gile.

"Nothing personal, just initiation."

The crowd is stunned by what they just witnessed.

CHAPTER 8:
Party's First Quest

Javier, Leo, Maya, Gile, and Elly sit at a table. There is awkward tension within the group.

"Look, that might not be the best way to introduce ourselves but I did heal you. I learned you guys can take a hit. Drinks and dinner are also on me," Javier says.

Elly gives a suggestive look to Javier. He sighs.

"I'm sorry. I'll reflect on my actions and be more mindful," he says in an unenthusiastic tone.

"No respect from a so-called Hero. How unsightly," Leo says.

"That did come by surprise, but water under the bridge," Gile says.

"Isn't that forgiving too easily?" Maya asked.

"Sometimes it's easier to go along with things than question them," Gile replies.

"Well, I refuse to work with a dirty peasant on his high horse because he is the hero!" Leo yells.

Javier has his hand on his gun.

"How about we settle down?" Elly says, trying to de-escalate the situation.

"I'm sorry, but who are you?" Maya asks.

"Oh right, this is Elly. She's my receptionist and starting today, she's yours as well," Javier interrupts.

Gile sits there bewitched by Elly's beauty.

"Hello," Leo said.

"Nice to have another woman within the group," Maya says.

"Nice to meet you all. Your matches were very impressive," Elly responded.

Gile is still staring at Elly. Elly notices. She clears her throat.

"Anyways, I have a quest specifically asking for the Hero. It says a group of children were kidnapped to be sold to slave traders."

"What?" Javier asked in disgust.

He looks at the quest form.

"Those poor children must be terrified," Maya says.

"We should leave soon before it's too late!" Gile says.

A carriage is moving along in the woods. In the carriage there are 15 children and a man with a dagger. Two men are up front, steering the carriage and being on the lookout.

"Soon enough we'll be living large!" one man says.

"All the booze and women's money can buy!" the other man says.

The children are crying and scared.

"Shut up! I hate babysitting," the man in the carriage says.

The two men up front are laughing.

Javier is making a circle with his hand up to his eye. He

turns to the rest.

"Big guy, can you use 'Stomp' to hit the carriage?" he asks.

"Huh? Isn't that risking the children's safety?" Gile questions.

"How pitiful. 'Switch'," Leo says as he rushes out towards the carriage.

"What are you? Damn it! Maya, follow him! Gile, you're with me!"

Maya sprints towards Leo. Leo swings his sword, sending an air slash towards the driver. The driver ducks as the other man gets hit and flies off the carriage.

"What the hell?" the driver said.

Maya throws her wand puncturing the driver's arm, causing him to lose control of his steering and swerve. He regains control, but Javier and Gile are waiting further down the path.

"Cut the tree!" Javier tells Gile.

Gile cuts the tree and it falls over, cutting off the path for the carriage. The driver yanks the horse's rope, making an immediate stop. The party rushes the carriage. The two men up front were captured. Javier then pushes Leo.

"What the hell was that?" Javier asked in anger.

Leo didn't answer.

The man in the carriage is holding a girl hostage, holding his dagger up to her neck. "If you don't want to be the reason she dies, then all of you back away, and let us go!"

Javier sucks his teeth, rolls his eyes, and shoots the man in his ear. The man let go of the girl. Javier shoots him again in his leg. He then proceeds to shoot his other leg and both arms. The man can no longer move his limbs. Javier holds the gun against the man's cranium.

"Now then, where were you taking them?" Javier asks.

"Go to hell."

Javier laughs. "You can go first."

Suddenly the man closes his eyes and a growl comes from deeper within the woods.

"Albino Wolves!" Gile yells.

"BANG" one wolf goes down.

"CLICK" "You can't be serious," Javier says.

"Water Cage!" Maya chants.

The two wolves stop and are temporarily immobilized.

"You can reload using earth magic," Javier remembers Aisha explaining.

He puts his hand to his gun . He seems confused.

"How am I supposed to 'Reload'?" the gun glows.

Javier checks the gun; It's fully loaded.

"BANG" "BANG" the two wolves go down as well.

Javier turns to the man on the ground again.

"I'm still not talking!" the man says.

"Yeah, I figured. I've grown impatient. I have something better in mind," Javier smirks.

The party drives the carriage back into the Royal Capital and the three men tied to the back of the carriage are dragged along. The men were turned in and the children were released from the carriage and their shackles. They line the children up to be healed.

"The families thank you, the children will be returned to their homes. Good work heroes," the soldier said.

He hands the reward to Javier.

"All right! Now that it's over, I'm heading to my room. Elly will split the reward, you can come for it later," Javier said.

As he turns to walk away, he feels a tug on his pants. He turns and sees a little girl in a hood.

"Tha..ou..." she says in a broken voice.

"Uh yeah," Javier says to the girl.

"She seems fond of you," Maya says.

"Right," he awkwardly says.

He kneels and says, "Hey, don't you want to see your fam?"

Her hair is white and her eyes are crimson red.

"Javier?" Gile is concerned.

"I got to go. She's coming with me, I happen to know her," Javier rushes off to the guild. He spots Elly and signals her over to his room.

Javier checks to make sure no one is close enough to hear and shuts the door.

"We might have a problem," Javier says.

Elly looks confused. Javier slowly pulls the little girl's hood down.

Elly is in shock. "A demon?" she asks.

The girl gets scared and backs up into a wall.

"Hey, It's okay. No one is going to hurt you here," he assures her.

The demon girl is shaking but inches toward Javier.

"Do you have a name?" Elly asks.

"L..ly," the girl says brokenly.

"Can you talk louder?" he asks.

"Hur... to...alk" the girl says.

Javier and Elly look at each other.

"Heal!" Javier chants while holding his gun. He points at Lily.

"BANG" light surrounds Lily. All her scars disappear.

"Try to speak," Javier said.

"My name is Lily."

She is shocked that she's speaking normally without feeling pain.

Elly sighs in relief.

"Lily, where is your family?" Javier asks.

"Family?" she begins tearing up.

"Got it. Well, would you like to stay with me?" Javier asked.

"Huh?" Elly and Lily both question.

"I don't know if that is a good idea Javi," Elly said.

"I had a daughter before. You know that," he responds.

"That's not the problem," Elly says.

"What, she's a demon? Who cares? Lily, would you like to stay with me?"

Lily seems unsure. She thinks for a minute.

"Yes," she says in a shy voice.

"Alright then. It's settled."

Elly gets worried about what's to come.

"Don't worry. She'll stay with me," Javier assures her.

"That worries me more."

In the middle of the night whilst everyone was sleeping, Lily woke up from a nightmare. She screamed, waking up Javier in panic. Javier looked at her and wrapped his arms around her to calm her down.

"Shh, calm down. It's okay. You're okay," Javier whispers to her.

Lily slowly calms down and holds Javier tightly. Javier wipes her tears and shushes her. Lily lies against Javier's side as he holds on. Javier is reminded of when his daughter used to have nightmares.

"What the hell?" Javier thought as Lily and Javier eventually slept.

CHAPTER 9:
A New Member

Both Javier and Aisha are having a civil conversation about what has happened recently.

"Are you out of your mind?" Aisha asks angrily.

"Huh?"

"You took in a demon. Why would you do that?"

Javier sighs. "You know I had a daughter."

"So you're replacing her? What's next? You're going to marry the elf to replace your wife?"

"What? No, she doesn't have a family to return to and I can relate to that from my past. I'll watch over her until I defeat the Demon Lord."

"Javi, this is a very terrible idea. If they find out you have a demon with you, they'll think you're working undercover."

"Look, I came to you to see if you had any way to hide her identity. I'm not going to push her away. You also weren't exactly helpful with learning magic," Javier argues.

Aisha gets irritated. She sighs.

"There is a special magic spell you can cast. You use your

light magic that can change her hair color."

"What about her eyes?" Javier asks.

"Same spell."

"Okay, what is the spell?"

"That is for you to figure out."

"Huh?"

"I can't tell you how to do everything. Also this is your mess; you handle the consequences. Check out the library and study up on magic. It isn't that hard."

"But, I don't have time for textbooks with demons trying to start a war!"

"You have your special ability."

"I didn't even know about special abilities until Elly explained it to me."

Aisha playfully smiles. Javier sighs.

"What's my special ability?"

"Copycat. You can see something or learn something once and can copy it to an exact recreation. You add it to your arsenal."

Javier grins. "Alright, that could work."

"Time to wake up, Hero. You must be careful; the path you're taking is quite thorny. Until we meet again," Aisha said.

Javier and Lily meet for breakfast with the rest of the party.

"So basically she's now one of us," Javier explains without mentioning she is a demon.

"Why not take her to an orphanage?" Leo asks.

"They're not as comfortable as you'd think. Of course, you wouldn't know about those in classes under you and how they live," Javier says.

"Incompetence."

"What's your deal?" Javier asks, annoyed.

"I'm not quite sure what you mean."

"You know what I'm talking about. You always have something to say. So what's your problem?"

"I don't accept you as the Hero. You're just a dirty, incompetent, poor excuse of a hero."

"Maybe we should calm down," Elly says.

"Right, we should focus more on defeating the Demon Lord," Gile says.

"My, you boys have such short tempers."

Javier and Leo glare at each other and then look away.

"Lily is part of our group now, end of discussion," Javier says.

"Lily? She is quite the young one. I'm Maya."

"Hello, I'm Gile."

Leo looks at Lily. "I am Leo."

Lily is covering herself with her hood.

Elly feels relieved things are calming down.

"Or four eyes," Javier said.

Or so she thought. Leo slammed a fist onto the table. The entire restaurant got quiet and stared.

"Look out, wannabe 'Hero' and the 'Failed Noble' are about to cause mayhem!" a drunk man said.

"Oh boy," Gile said.

Leo grabs his sword, then Javier grabs Leo's wrist.

"Don't," Javier warns Leo.

Leo gets irritated but eventually lets go of his sword.

"Apologies for the noise. Allow me to pay for your table's bill," Javier said.

"That's more like it. Maybe you aren't as troubled as I thought. Too bad your choice of members is poor," he said.

Javier doesn't respond but forces a smile.

"Especially a child. Are you desperate?"

"Elly, please take Lily to the dorms. Javier says, clenching his teeth.

Elly and Lily leave.

"Now, what's your name?"

"Rodger, you can also refer to me as one of the best adventures from the Royal Capital back in the day."

"Okay Rodger, I don't appreciate you talking badly about my party."

"Well excuse me! You have a failed noble, slutty witch, and a meathead. Don't even get me started on that elf playing mother to the abandoned child," Rodger says drunkenly.

Javier gets a mug from the waitress. He walks towards Rodger.

"Well, you know drinking alcohol in the morning isn't good for you?" Javier pours the alcohol on Rodger.

Everyone but Javier is shocked. He gets in Rodger's face and glares.

"I don't care what you think of me, but don't you dare say anything about my group unless you're ready to get put in the ground," Javier threatens.

"What?" Rodger questions.

Javier breaks the wooden mug over Rodger's head and punches him out of his seat. The two men Rodger was eating with got up to fight. Leo stood next to Javier.

"They're mine," Leo said.

Javier grabbed the edge of the table and flipped it. Punches are being thrown, tables are flipped; A full-on brawl broke out. Javier's eyes wander around, seeing the chaos. Gile is wrestling with someone.

"I'm not looking for trouble," Gile said.

"Damn it, Gile! I chose you because you're strong! Show me the power you have!" Javier yelled.

Gile's face got serious. He picks up the guy and tosses him across the restaurant. Javier looks for Maya. Maya is on top of a man's shoulders forming water in his face.

"Switch!" Leo chanted and his sword turned wooden. He was fighting the men who were drinking with Rodger. Rodger gets up from the ground and runs towards Javier to tackle him. Javier puts his gun up in Rodger's face. Rodger froze.

"Got you" Javier said mockingly and then proceeded to punch him, knocking him out.

The Hero's party was fighting everyone in the restaurant. Royal guards enter because of the noise.

"Stop!" a guard yells.

Everyone stops.

"Who is responsible for this?" the guard asked.

Everyone steps away from Javier and Leo.

"God damn it," Javier says.

They were taken to jail and are now sitting in a cell.

"I can't believe you got us thrown in a cell!" Leo said.

"You were willing to swing first."

"What difference does it make?"

"Then you would've started it."

"Well, we still ended up here."

"Relax, Elly will get us out," Javier said as he got in a push-up position. He starts doing push-ups.

"So tell me, what's with the whole 'Failed Noble' thing? You seem pretty skilled overall, except for listening," Javier asks.

"Like I must explain myself to you."

"We're in the same group now. I watch your back, and you watch mine. I don't care if you like me or not. I don't know how I feel about you but I can at least respect you."

Leo sighs.

"When I was eleven, I was considered extremely talented. I was exceptional in sword-wielding and academics. I was praised and had quite a confidence boost. My family and I went on a trip to another city. Bandits ambushed us. The bandits looked a lot like demons. I heard conspiracy that deals were made with demons but never saw one in the flesh."

"What kind of deals?"

"They sacrifice part of their humanity for demon abilities."

Javier stops doing push-ups. He gets up and sits on the bench.

"My brothers and I were told to stay in the carriage. My parents and guards were fending off against the bandits. I ran out trying to help considering I was talented. My confidence was masking my ignorance. There was one left and he ran towards me. As he was about to attack me, my mother jumped in front of me, sacrificing herself. Ever since then, I've been called the 'Failed Noble.' At first it was only my brothers and my father. Then it became other nobles saying I'm responsible for my mother's death," Leo sits there in sadness.

Javier looks at Leo. Javier gets flashbacks of when his family was killed. The trip to the hospital and his wife's family blaming Javier for their deaths.

"But it's not your fault," Javier said.

"How is it not?"

"It was out of your hands. Sure, you shouldn't have gone out, but let's say your brothers went out instead. It would be the same outcome."

"But..."

"Look, I get how it looks, but they're just hurt from losing a loved one. They're looking for someone to blame. I went through the same thing."

"Oh please, whose death were you blamed for?" Leo asked, fighting tears.

"My wife and daughter. I was nearby when it happened and couldn't do anything to stop it. My wife's family blamed me and cut contact completely after the funeral. That eventually led to how I became the hero."

"Demons killed your family?"

"Not really but I don't care who it was. I wanted revenge.

It didn't go as planned and now I'm here."

"Well, I'm sorry for your loss," Leo said.

"Yeah. Like I said, you're skilled. It was mainly why I picked you. Also the King pisses me off and you beating his son was satisfying."

Leo and Javier chuckle.

"Defeating the Demon Lord is my main goal. I'll prove that I'm not a failure," Leo said.

"We're a team, we all have our reasons. Let's kick that demon's ass."

A guard approaches and opens the cell.

"You're free to go, you've been bailed out. Please try not to cause more trouble, Hero."

Javier and Leo were met with the rest of the group. Lily hugs Javier.

"How did you afford to bail us out so fast?" Leo asks.

"From Javi's secret stash. He made a lot from his solo quests," Elly replied.

Javier puts his weapons away.

"Damn it. How much?" Javier asks.

"Let's go," Elly says.

"Elly, how much?," Javier asks while following Elly.

To this day Javier still has not found out how much Elly spent.

CHAPTER 10:
Lessons and Deals

(Part 1)

The group was having breakfast at the guild diner.

"Hey boss, I'm not one to start trouble but I've noticed you haven't initiated Lily," Gile says.

Lily and Javier look at each other confused.

"You want me to punch a little girl?" Javier questions.

"What? No, it's just..." Gile stutters.

"Relax, I'm joking," Javier chuckles.

Javier looks at Lily and proceeds to flick her in the forehead, holding back his hero strength. Lily covers her head in pain. Elly coddles her.

"Javi!" Elly said in shock.

"I do believe we haven't seen Elly initiated either," Maya mentioned.

Elly looks at Javier. Javier raises his hand and Elly flinches. He pats Elly's head.

"I'm not hitting her. She's different. Plus I made her cry a while back."

Elly blushes and is embarrassed.

"Ew, they're flirting," Lily said.

"What? We're not..." Elly says flustered.

"Just teasing," Javier said.

"What is on the agenda today?" Leo asks.

"Right, so after what happened yesterday, It'd be ideal if we laid low for a bit; you have the day off today. Just try not to get arrested again," Javier responded.

"You were arrested Javi," Lily said.

He pats Lily's head, "That's right, but I was fighting bad guys."

The group splits up. Javier and Lily went to the library. Javier picked up some books about magic and some picture books for Lily. As Javier reads, he's adding spells to his arsenal.

"What are you reading Javi?" Lily asks.

"I'm learning about magic. Do you know how to use magic?"

Lily nods no.

"I heard you need mana," Lily said.

"Mana?" Javier looks confused.

"Oh my, Hero?" Maya noticed.

"Maya?"

Maya walks over and sits across from Javier.

"What brings you here?" Javier asks.

"I tend to spend my spare time at libraries," Maya responds.

"Do you like reading Maya?" Lily asks.

Maya pats Lily's head, "Yes, knowledge is quite valuable. For instance, you were confused about mana. Mana is the magic energy that flows within you. The more mana you have, the stronger the magic is. Since you're the hero, your magic must be powerful," Maya explains.

"What about you? Your file said you're a Multi-Caster. If you ask me, that's a pretty impressive skill," Javier says.

"Well of course," Maya says in arrogance.

Maya grabs Javier's hands.

"Most magic users let the mana flow to one hand or use both for one spell. I chant one spell, releasing my mana to one hand and mentally cast another spell while delaying the mana release in the other," Maya explains.

"I see. Care for a little one-on-one sparring? I want to see it up close," Javier suggests.

"Oh my, how bold of you to ask such a thing from a woman," Maya says.

"I was talking about your ability."

Maya leans into Javier's ear.

"I was as well. Don't be shy however, I wouldn't mind showing more than my ability."

Javier flicks Maya in the forehead with a bit more force than against Lily.

"Javi is flirting again," Lily says.

"Let's just spar," Javier says.

Javier and Maya are at the training field where the matches take place. They stand twenty feet apart. Elly and Lily are watching from a distance. Maya quickly threw her wand at Javier. He dodges it and chants "Stone Bullet!" Maya slides underneath it and charges at Javier. "Fireball!" she chants and throws as she creates a diagonal wall of ice. She jumps on the wall and swiftly slides towards Javier. He rolls forward and pulls out his gun. He fires in front of Maya. He chants, "Reload!" She loses her balance and jumps off but sinks into the ground.

Maya is confused while Javier grins.

"Got you," Javier says, smirking.

"Is that so?" she replies.

Javier looks confused.

"Expand!" Maya chants and the hole widens, freeing Maya. She also whips Javier with a water spell.

Javier pulls out his knife and slashes at Maya. She swiftly dodges and evades his attacks. She kicks the knife out of his hand and jumps on top of Javier's shoulders. She punches him in the face. Javier jumps and drops on Maya. Maya released her grip out of pain.

"Lightning Strike!" Javier chants.

A bolt of lightning strikes down. Maya braces for impact.

"CRASH" the lightning echoed.

Maya is unharmed. The lightning struck a foot away from her. She sees Javier walking away, picking up her wand and his knife. She gets up. Javier hands her wand over.

"What happened?" Maya asked.

"What do you mean?" he asks, confused.

"Why didn't it hit me?"

"I won. You would've probably died. Do you think I'd

actually strike you with lightning in a sparring match? If we were fighting for real, I would. We're party members, I can't have you dying on me. Are you hurt anywhere?"

Maya shows her back where she landed.

"Heal!" Javier chants.

"BANG" "BANG" Javier heals Maya and himself.

"This is the first time I noticed. You have a lot of tattoos," Javier mentioned.

"W-Well, I'll admit defeat today," Maya says slightly flustered.

"Maya is flirting!" Lily said from a distance.

"You're mistaken Lily!" Maya says flustered.

Maya and Javier meet with Elly and Lily.

"I must do work, so I'm going to the guild. Please watch over her," Elly says.

She says bye to the others.

Maya starts walking away. Javier stops her, catching her by surprise. She gets suddenly nervous.

"Do you know anything about making deals with demons?" Javier asks.

Maya sighed and composed herself.

"Not too much. Why do you ask?"

"I heard about it recently and had questions."

"I know a shopkeeper who knows more about such matters."

"Can you take me to him?"

"I don't think we should take Lily."

"Either way I have to meet this guy and possibly with the result, I'll need her with me," Javier said.

"Result?"

There was a slight pause. Maya and Javier stare at each other.

"Let's just go," Javier says.

They enter a small shop that has dim lighting.

"Stay close to me, Lily," Javier says, holding her hand.

"It's harmless, for the most part," Maya says as she rings the desk bell.

A man walks out from the back room and towards the counter.

"Hello, Maya? To what do I owe the pleasure?" he says.

"Nothing this time but he has questions," Maya says pointing at Javier.

"The Hero?" the man backs against the wall.

"Whatever you heard, it is not true!" the shopkeeper said.

"What? No, I have questions about demons and making deals," Javier said.

"Making deals with demons?" the shopkeeper asked.

CHAPTER 11:
Lessons and Deals

(Part 2)

"Making deals with demons?" the shopkeeper asked.

The man closes his shop. He walks towards his back room. He has the group follow him. They enter the room and see the lair of books and chemicals. The man closes the curtain to the entryway and he looks to see if anyone is around.

"What is it you're looking to know?"

"If I were to make a deal with a demon, what would happen and how would I do it?" Javier asks.

The man hesitates "This is top secret; not a word of this leaves this room or to the public."

The group agrees.

"Alright, first off, my name is Doctor Fern," the man says.

"He's not a doctor, but it's much easier to comply," Maya said.

"Javier," he points to Lily, "Lily."

"Nice to meet ya. Moving on, making deals with demons.

It's a big risk to one's humanity. The deal grants them demon abilities and battles the human conscience. Losing the battle could result in becoming 100% a mindless demon or in some cases, death. Fern said.

"How does one defeat the demon conscience before it takes over?" Javier asks.

"I narrowed it down to three ways. The first is being as pure as light and pleading with god to reject the conscience. The second way is having ill intentions and the demon inside allows control. The third way is this," he says holding a ring.

"What is it?" Lily asks.

"This ring is a catalyst that can maintain the demon's DNA to not overtake your body."

"Does it work?" Javier asks.

"Unfortunately I'm unsure. I haven't tested it and with the risk it could be, I'm not bold enough to risk myself," Fern said.

There was a slight pause.

"What about me?" Javier asks.

Maya and Lily are concerned.

"Hmm. Well I suppose I could, but if the Hero were to become a demon if it were to fail," Fern says unsure.

"I should be fine," Javier says.

Fern looks at Maya.

"This hero is quite the character."

"So? What do you say Doc?"

"Well, if we were to obtain a demon or demon DNA to test the ring. It doesn't come easily," Fern says.

"And if I were to have access to a demon?" Javier says.

Doctor Fern is intrigued. Javier turns to Maya.

"Maya this stays between you and me."

"Lily is a demon?" Maya confirms.

"How do you...?"

"I can tell. I am a witch afterall," Maya says.

Fern walks towards Lily.

"Really? Could I examine?"

Javier pulls Lily behind him.

"Let me make this clear. You don't touch Lily. You don't tell anyone about Lily. If you in any way, shape, or form harm or trouble comes her way, I won't hesitate to end your existence," Javier says glaring at Fern.

Fern puts his hands up and steps away.

"Alright, I understand," he says.

Javier turns to Lily and kneels.

"Lily, are you okay with making a deal with me?" Javier asks.

"I don't want you to get hurt, Javi," Lily says.

"It'll be fine. It will sting a little but it will be okay," Javier assures her.

"Okay," Lily replies.

Fern grabs a syringe.

"To be the most effective way, injection of demon blood," Fern said.

"How is that making a deal?" Javier asked.

"You make a deal as you have an intake of demon DNA."

Maya grabs the syringe from Fern.

"Javi, are you sure this is the brightest idea?" Maya asks.

Javier hesitates, "I'm never sure. I don't know how strong the Demon Lord is, but this might give me an advantage."

"If you think this is the way to go; I'm with you," Maya says.

"Maya, if anything were to go wrong," Javier says, looking at Maya.

Maya nods. She kneels next to Lily. Lily is scared. Javier kneels next to her, holding her hand.

"What was your book about?" Javier asked.

Lily's attention was on Javier and his question.

"Animals," Lily responded.

"Do you like animals?"

Lily nods.

"What is your favorite animal?"

"Cats."

"Okay, after this do you want to look at cats?"

"Yeah!" Lily said excitedly.

"Alright, it's done," Maya said.

"Heal!" Javier chanted.

"BANG" he heals Lily.

Fern looks at her curiously.

"What a strange item," Fern said.

"Alright, what now?" Javier asks.

"Right, over here," Fern says, directing Javier to a wall.

Fern straps Javier across his chest, right arm, and legs.

"A bit much don't you think?" Javier asks.

"As I mentioned before, it could fail. Part of me believes that your Hero strength won't be enough to hold," Fern responds.

Lily walks up to Javier. She grabs his free hand. Javier smiles at Lily to assure her that he was alright but inside he was getting nervous. Fern writes down the chant to make the deal. He gives it to Lily.

"Javier, do you look for demon abilities?" Lily reads.

Maya injects Javier with Lily's blood.

"Yes," Javier says.

"You shall be granted demon abilities, your humanity is however at risk. With that said... Fusion!" Lily chants.

Both Lily's and Javier's hands shine. They suddenly stop shining.

Maya pulls Lily away just in case it fails.

"How do you feel, Hero?" Fern asks.

"Javier begins shaking. Half his hair turned white, his left hand grew claws, and his left pupil turned crimson red. He yells in agony. He is getting flashbacks of his life in his old world.

"Don't worry, it's part of the process! I'll now place the ring!" Fern says inching towards Javier.

Javier swings at Fern. Fern steps back. Lily sneaks up and grabs Javier's demon hand. Javier looks at Lily. Lily is fighting tears.

"Javi!" Lily pleads.

Javi suddenly stops. He has calmed down a bit.

"My god," Fern says in disbelief.

"Fern!" Maya says.

Fern dashes to Javier and puts the ring on his demon finger. His hand slowly goes back to normal. His hair and eyes go back to their original color. Javier then passes out. Javier suddenly opens his eyes. He's not in the lair.

"Shit," Javier says, knowing what's about to happen.

"Javi! You can't be serious!" Javier hears from a distance.

"Look Aisha."

"No Javi, you look!" Aisha says in Javier's face.

"I get that it's not the smartest option, but I don't know how strong the Demon Lord is. This could give me an edge," Javier explains.

Aisha sighs.

"Javi, why do you do these things?"

"I did what you said. I studied magic, used my adaptation ability, and formed a party," Javier said.

"You also took in a demon, disrespected the King, and made a deal with a demon."

"Two things. One, that King can shove it. Secondly, I know it could cause trouble, but it will be fine."

"I'm starting to think you aren't the right choice for the Hero."

"Huh? My goal hasn't changed. I'm still going to fight the Demon Lord to claim my wish."

Aisha sighs again," as long as you haven't gone down the evil path, I'll allow you to continue. Please just stop being reckless."

"Don't worry, I got this," Javier says.

Aisha finds it hard to believe that.

"Time to wake up Hero, until we meet again," Aisha says.

Javier comes back to reality.

"Did it work?" Javier asked.

"Javi!" Lily yells running into Javier's free arm.

Maya breathes in relief.

"How do you feel now?" Fern asks.

"Fine. I spoke to the goddess for a bit, she's pissed, but I got the okay. Leo however, does not know about this," Javier says.

"Why?" Lily asks.

"Leo met bad guys who made deals and used their powers for evil. He'll think I'm a bad guy so we must keep this secret okay?"

Lily nods agreeing.

"Right! I will need you to come in for occasional check ups and research. Also I probably should have mentioned before that ring is attached to your finger. You can't get rid of it unless you also discard your finger," Fern says.

Javier sighs, "Sure, whatever," he said while looking at the ring.

He looks at Maya.

"You are being quiet, what's going through your head?"

"Javi you, you." Maya said, fighting tears.

Javier sighs and hugs Maya. Maya didn't expect that response from Javier.

"Don't get used to this. I didn't expect you to care so much about me. Still, Miss Confidence I won't judge you if you cry sometimes," he said teasingly.

He puts a hand on Lily's head, "Alright, let's go see those cats." Javier said.

CHAPTER 12:
Lily's First Quest

Javier, Lily, and Gile travel to a field to collect herbs.

"Can you explain to me why neither Leo nor Maya are coming and why Lily is?" Gile asked.

Javier explains the conversation an hour prior.

"Javi, can I go on a quest with you?" Lily asks.

Elly spits her tea out of shock.

Javier pauses, "Sure." he says.

"Javi!" Elly yells.

Javier looks at Elly in confusion.

"We're not sending Lily on a quest.

"Lily, you're 12 right?" Javier asks.

Lily nods no. She's 9 years old.

"Hmm, she's old enough to start adventuring. Besides, she'll be with me." Javier said.

"That worries me even more," Elly said.

"Huh? How?"

"Javi I understand you'd protect Lily but, how do I put this? You tend to do things in the most bizarre way. I'd rather Lily not pick up your habits." Elly explains.

"It'll be fine. I'll work on it."

"So you still plan on doing something crazy?"

Javier stays quiet.

"Take someone from the party with you and do an herb-collecting quest." Elly said.

Javier sighs. Javier spots Gile.

"Fine. Gile! We have a quest! Let's go!"

"What? Oh, okay." Gile responds.

"Happy?" Javier asks Elly.

"No, but Gile being there makes me a little less stressed and assured of Lily's safety." she says.

Javier rolls his eyes. While Gile prepares, the rest goes to get Lily's license printed. The license says Lily is 12 years old. Gile meets up with them and they head out.

"Stay out of trouble," Elly says.

"She'll be fine. Isn't that right Lily?" Javier said.

"I was talking to you," Elly responded.

Javier sucks his teeth.

Gile is up to speed.

"What about Leo and Maya?" Gile asks.

"Oh right, Leo had some family business to take care of and Maya, for some reason, is feeling sick. She refused to get out of bed today." Javier said.

Maya is in bed. She can't believe she cried in front of Javier.

"Still, I won't judge you if you cry sometimes, miss confidence," Maya remembers Javier saying. She gets embarrassed under her blanket.

"That man dares to embarrass me? He won't get away with that. I'll seduce him into submission." she says.

Javier sneezes.

"Are you sick too?" Gile asks.

"These damn flowers are everywhere!" Javier says.

Lily is enjoying the beauty of the scenery and the colors.

Javier pulls out a different knife from his usual knife.

"Here, this is for you Lily," Javier says, holding the knife.

"Uh boss, are you sure giving her a knife is a good idea?" Gile questions.

"Yes, she has to learn to fight and defend herself in emergencies. I also made sure it was made from mythril." Javier said.

"Mythril? How did you afford that?" Gile asked in shock.

"You calling me broke?" Javier said jokingly.

"N-no, I wasn't," Gile said nervously.

Javier starts laughing. Gile is awkwardly laughing.

Lily grabs the knife.

"No need to be scared of the knife, Lily. It's for protection. Just follow my lead, okay?" Javier said.

Lily nods. Javier demonstrates a few quick slashes. He then signals Lily to try. She imitates the slashes exactly how she was shown. Javier praises her.

"Just like that! Okay, here is a trick to get an advantage. You kick their knee inward so that they lose balance and lunge at your opponent while holding the knife with both hands." Javier says.

"Aren't we collecting herbs?" Gile asked.

Javier sighs, "Fine. Here Lily, this is a sheath for your knife. If you need to fight, pull it out." Javier says.

He puts the sheath on a belt for Lily to wear. He then pats her head.

"Alright, let's pick these herbs," Javier says unenthusiastically.

The three spend the next hour picking herbs.

"Alright, that should do it. We might have gotten too much," Javier said.

"That was fun," Lily said.

"Congratulations on completing your first quest, Miss Lily." Gile said.

Lily smiles. They begin walking towards the Royal Capital. They suddenly stop. They hear a noise that Javier is unfamiliar with. A group of goblins jump out from the bushes.

"God damn it, why does everything try to sneak attack?" Javier says while pulling his knife out.

"Gile guard Lily! Don't let any of them get near her!" Javier yelled.

"Right! Stay behind me Lily." Gile says.

Javier is killing the goblins but the number overwhelms him. Lily sees it and is getting worried. A goblin cuts Javier in the arm. He lets out a groan of pain.

"Javi!" Lily yells.

She pulls out the knife and rushes to Javier's aid.

"Lily!" Gile yells while chasing after her.

"No! Lily don't." Javier says.

Lily incredibly slashes goblins. The number is dropping every slash. Javier runs to Lily. They are back to back.

"Okay, you got guts. Let's do this!" Javier says.

"Right!" Lily responds while having an adrenaline rush.

Javier and Lily are slashing wildly. Gile starts swinging at goblins. There are a few left.

"Gile, stomp at me!" Javier yells.

Gile stomps. It rushes to Javier, he grabs a goblin's cranium and slams its skull into the part that rises, smashing the goblin's skull. There seems to be one left and Lily dashes towards it.

She swings, but it blocks. She is being overpowered.

"Lily, kick the knee!" Javier says while pulling his gun out.

Lily kicks the goblin's knee inward and clutches the knife with both hands. She drove the blade into the goblin's skull. It seemed it was over. One of the goblins was not completely dead. It got up and charged Lily.

The goblin's blade was an inch away from Lily's face when Javier knees the goblin in the jaw.

"BANG" "BANG" "BANG" Javier shoots both its arms and one of its legs. He ties a rope around its neck like a leash.

"Where did you get the rope?" Gile asks.

"Spatial Magic," Javier responded without taking his eyes off the goblin.

He stops and walks up to Lily and Gile. He casts heal on his gun and hands it to Gile.

"I'll be right back. I'll only need a minute." Javier says seriously.

"BANG" "BANG" both Gile and Lily are healed.

"What is Javi doing?" Lily asks.

"I'm not sure, he might..." Gile says.

"CRASH" "BOOM" "SPLASH" "STOMP"

For context, the "CRASH" was a lightning strike, followed by an explosive fireball, then a splash of water,and after that Javier stomped its skull with Hero strength. He comes back as if nothing happened.

Gile and Lily decide not to ask about it. Gile returns Javier's gun back.

"BANG" Javier heals himself.

"Let's go," Javier said.

"Wait, we can make money off of them. It's Ten Marbs per ear," Gile said.

"Sure but, one goblin might not be useful," Javier says as he looks at the forest.

"R-Right," Gile said.

They returned to town and claimed their reward. They got a total of 300 Marbs off the goblin ears alone. Adding the reward for the quest is a total of 425 Marbs. Elly welcomes them back. Javier is carrying Lily on his back.

"Is Lily alright?" Elly asks urgently.

"She's fine. She just fell asleep." Javier said.

Elly feels relieved.

"Well, I'm going to shower. I can't stand the smell of those goblins." Gile said.

"God damn it Gile," Javier mumbled.

Javier went to put Lily in bed. After he sets Lily down, he feels a tight grip on his shoulder. It was Elly.

"Goblins, huh?" Elly asked with a terrifying aura.

Javier felt chills down his spine but recomposed himself.

"We were ambushed, but we took care of it. We got a pretty good payment also." Javier responded.

Elly sees the new knife on the nightstand.

"What's wrong with your original knife?" she asked.

"What are you talking about?" Javier asked, confused.

Elly points out the knife. Javier places his palm in his face. Elly went to slap Javier but he grabbed both of her wrists. He sighs.

"Lily needs to learn how to defend herself," he said.

"She's only a child," Elly said.

"Who's skilled!" he responded.

"You let her fight monsters?" Elly asked angrily.

Javier stayed quiet. Elly stares at Javier.

"Look, you know more than anyone I won't be here forever. I want to make sure Lily will be alright when I leave." Javier stated.

"I know, I know, but..." Elly said in sorrow.

"We're together until the end. In this case, it's defeating the Demon Lord. Things will work out."

Lily heard almost everything. She felt upset hearing that but decided to pretend to be sleeping.

CHAPTER 13:
Dragon Hot Spring

(Part 1)

The entire party is eating dinner. Javier puts six tickets on the table.

"We're going on a trip," Javier says.

The party seemed confused by the sudden announcement.

"Where?" Lily asks.

"I got us tickets to the legendary 'Black Dragon Hot Spring'."

"Hot spring?" everyone simultaneously said.

"I figured we've been working and training for a while. Lily completed her first quest not too long ago. It's always good to relax every once in a while," Javier said.

The group saw his point.

"Hot Spring? Poor Javi has no clue that's where he could fall for seduction easily. It's time for some revenge," Maya thought.

"Hot Spring? It could be good to relax and clear my head after visiting my family," Leo thought.

"Hot Spring, huh? I wonder if I can convince some ladies

to join me in the mixed bath area," Gile thought.

"Javier had done a lot recently that was utter chaos. It's nice to see him sit back and we can have a peaceful weekend," Elly thought.

"I've never been to a Hot Spring. That sounds exciting," Lily thought.

"We're in," the group said.

"Alright, we'll leave in the morning," Javier said.

"After talking to that crazy doc, I can learn to use my demon abilities. Thank god I can use their open space with a mountain between us. I have to make sure they're unaware of my abilities," Javier thought.

Javier remembers his latest check up with Doctor Fern.

"So, how do you use my demon abilities with this on?" Javier asked.

"Well, if you see Hero, you can see different variations. There are three different settings within the ring. You twist the ring and it changes its level. Level 1 is 25% of your demon power. Level 2 is 50% of your demon power. The third level is 75% of your power. Never start with 75% because that could destroy the ring with all that power releasing at once," Fern said.

"Wait, how do I go 100%?" Javier asked.

"That would require you to take off the ring, but that is very risky to your whole being. The ring does conserve the demonic DNA, but at 100% it could still take over and can be the end of you," Fern said.

Javier is disappointed.

"So, how do you know for sure? You said you haven't tested it. For someone who claimed to have never seen it, you know too much. What are you hiding?" Javier suspects.

"Oh, please. This is helping with my research. I've studied so much material about deals and demons. I'm continuing the research of geniuses of the past. You should learn how to use your limited power before going all at once. It increases your dark magic and forbidden magic."

"Forbidden magic?"

"Yes, it's spells that are lost in time however; they were at one point illegal. Not many were able to use such magic, but you have the power of the Hero and demon DNA, so you might be able to use it. It is rumored to curse the user, however."

"As fun as that sounds, I'll hold off on the forbidden magic," Javier said in concern.

Fern gives Javier a book full of Fern's notes on dark magic and forbidden magic.

"You explained your special ability is adaptation. I'm lending you this book to learn magic for both darkness and forbidden magic. You may choose not to use forbidden magic, but it's still useful knowledge. Once you learn everything from the book, you must return it to me. Forbidden magic isn't in books about magic in any library in the country, that makes it much more valuable. Dark magic is partially common but this book holds spells that are not known to humans."

"Noted," Javier said as he put the book away.

With that being what Javier learned before the trip, it is

now morning and they are off to the Hot Spring resort. Around evening they arrive and check in.

"We're here for three days and two nights, do what you will," Javier said.

The group splits up. The girls are taking advantage of the bath and the men go their separate ways. Leo is enjoying his time in the men's bath. Gile is chatting with some female residents of the resort, along with being shot down. Javier is on his way around the mountain.

Elly is cleaning Lily.

"So Elly, what is your relationship with Javi?" Maya asks.

Elly wasn't expecting that question.

"What do you mean?" Elly asks.

"Us women of the group haven't interacted much without the men. I figured we would bond and get to know each other a bit more," Maya responds.

"Oh, I'm fine with that."

They move to the Hot Spring afterward.

"So, what is your relationship with Javi? You two seem rather close," Maya questioned.

"I was one of the first people he met. He was registering for an adventurer's license in the town where I was stationed. I was transferred to the Royal Capital to help out Javi. He was the same troublemaker he is now but he is determined. I like to think of us as good friends," Elly said genuinely.

"I see, so you're not lovers?"

"L-Lovers? No, not at all," Elly gets flustered.

"What about you? What are your thoughts on Javi?" Elly asks.

Maya was a little shocked but kept her composure, "Javi is quite the trouble maker as he makes some of the most unique decisions. I respect him, though. He's pretty dependable at times and very strong. He seems very fatherly with Lily as well."

"True, he did talk about having a daughter before," Elly said.

"Huh? A daughter? He has a child?" Maya asks, shocked.

"Well, there's not much I can say because I promised him not to tell anyone. It's not my place to say anything on that topic," Elly explained.

Maya is taken aback. She realizes there is more to Javier than she thought.

"I wonder if that's why he hasn't fallen for my seductive charm," Maya says.

"I'm not sure."

"So you haven't thought about it? You're just friends?"

"Just friends."

"Well, other than a receptionist, I don't know anything about you. What brought you to be a receptionist?" Maya asked.

"I was always fascinated by the adventurer lifestyle. It was always exciting. I wanted to be in that field after I quit being an adventurer. My party leader became the guild leader of my old town," Elly said.

"My, you were an adventurer? I never would've guessed."

"Yes, but that's in the past. I stopped when we lost some of our members to a quest. Five of us left, two of us returned back alive."

"Oh my, I'm sorry to hear that."

"Thank you. It's ancient history. I was much younger and more rebellious," Elly said.

"You, rebellious? I don't see it."

"I was referred to as the 'Foul Elf.' Most thought of me as a delinquent."

"Elly, what is a delinquent?" Lily asked.

Elly hesitated, "A delinquent is a bad person. They don't listen to rules and say bad words."

"You're not a bad person. You're a nice person," Lily said.

"My, am I a good person Lily?" Maya asked.

"You're nice, Javi said you were a nice, pretty lady," Lily responded.

Maya began to turn red.

"I see," Maya said with slight shock.

"Who knew Javi would compliment your looks while having a wife?" Elly said with slight annoyance in her voice.

"Oh my, is that jealousy?" Maya asked.

There was a slight pause.

"Wife?!" Maya thought.

"W-What? No way!" Elly responded.

The girls start laughing.

"What about you? Were you an adventurer before this party?" Elly asked.

"I suppose. I did solo quests and never really had a party except a few other times. I joined this one party for a quest and they said they don't appreciate my seductive uniform in front of their boyfriends and how I don't stay behind the front line to cast spells," Maya said.

"I had a question about that. You're a witch so you're powerful with magic, but you also fight in hand-to-hand combat. Plus the sharpened knife. Why is that?" Elly asked.

"Oh well, because I'm a witch I don't need a wand. They are mainly for beginner magic control. As you saw in my match and spar with Javi, I use it as a slashing weapon and weaken the opponent before my next attack. I learned hand-to-hand combat thinking it could be useful. Most magic users are fighting at a distance meaning, if an opponent gets up close, fighting with magic gets difficult," Maya said.

"I use a slashing weapon too," Lily said.

"Is that so?" Maya said, looking at Elly.

"Javi," Elly said.

Maya was no longer shocked.

"Speaking of which, I wonder what he's up to?" Maya said.

Javier sneezes.

"These damn plants!" he said.

"Okay, Level 3."

He places his hand on the ground and chants "Summon Wolf" and an all-black wolf is summoned. Javi pets it.

"I'm kicking that demon's ass," Javi said.

Suddenly the ground shakes. The wolf vanishes. Javier looks up and he is covered in a huge shadow. Javier is in clear shock at what he saw. He reset his ring and made his way to the resort.

A giant bell was being rung.

"Get inside! We're under attack!" a man yelled.

The girls and guys get ready quickly and rush outside. Javier uses his spatial magic to teleport to the resort. He meets up with them upfront.

"What's going on?" Elly yelled.

"Well..." Javier was cut off by a deafening roar.

Javier points up. The group looks and is in shock.

"We have to do something! Everyone's lives are in danger!" Gile said.

They see a huge black dragon.

Javier sighs, "It just had to be a dragon, didn't it?"

CHAPTER 14:
Dragon Hot Springs

(Part 2)

"It just had to be a dragon?" Javier said, upset.

"Everyone in!" The man yelling has Javier yanking on his collar."

"Gather everyone in one room! Maya, Leo, Gile; distract the dragon and lead it away from the resort!" Javier said.

"What are you doing?" Elly said.

A few minutes later, all residents and employees are in the diner hall. Javier chants, "Portal!" And a portal opens.

"Everyone inside now! Elly, take Lily with you. Don't worry this portal takes you to the guild. We'll take care of it," Javier said.

Elly takes Lily with her and trusts the party will get the job done.

Javier rushes over to the rest of his party. They got the dragon to go the opposite direction but they're cornered. The dragon used its fire breath, but luckily, Maya made a shield using water just in time. Javier shoots at the dragon. The dragon now focuses on Javier. Leo rushes towards Javier "Switch!" he chanted.

"Javi, shoot magic at me quickly!" Leo yelled.

Javier didn't waste any time throwing explosive fireballs at Leo. Leo's sword absorbed them. Leo slashed up at the dragon and Javier's fireballs were coming out at a faster pace and dealt extra damage. The dragon took damage from it.

"I have an idea! Gile, come with me. Maya, use your magic to fill Leo's sword while attacking the dragon!" Javier said.

"Right!" the rest said.

Javier and Gile went up the mountain with a portal.

"What are we doing up here?" Gile asked.

Javier chanted "Expand!" and the mountain expanded out a flat platform.

"Okay, the dragon is going to get led here. When you're above it, you're going to jump off and swing your axe as hard as you can," Javier explained.

"Um, I don't think I can..." Gile got interrupted.

"Gile! You're strong! Show me why I picked you!" Javier yelled in his face.

Gile was still unsure but decided to go and said, "Let's do this!"

"Lead the dragon here!" Javier yelled as he shot at the dragon again. The dragon didn't get phased because it was far.

"Damn it, a hand gun won't do much from here!" Javier thought. He sees Maya and Leo fending off the dragon. "Switch!" Leo chanted. Javier thought of something. He put his hand on his gun and chanted "Switch!" and his gun started glowing. It turned into a sniper rifle. Gile is shocked and Javier grins. He carefully aim's for a dragon's eye and shoots it. The dragon turns and focuses on Javier. Javier jumps down the mountain and lands to the bottom. The dragon gets close and Gile jumps. He lets out a giant scream as he swings his axe. The dragon's scales barely cracked. Gile was falling and Maya sent a gust of wind to let him land safely.

"Lightning Strike!" Javier chanted. The lightning bolt dealt significant damage to the dragon. The dragon lands on the ground. Javier rushes the dragon. He jumps on the dragon. The dragon went berserk. Excessively breathing fire and jumping around. Javier was launched up. Javier casts heal on his gun and throws it towards his group. The dragon opened its mouth and Javier went in its mouth.

"Javi!" Maya yelled.

"No!" Gile yelled.

"You bastard! You'll pay for this!" Leo yelled.

The three run towards the dragon ready to unleash all they had left. Then suddenly "CRASH" "BOOM" "CRASH" "BOOM."

Lighting was attacking the dragon from above and the dragon was being exploded from the inside. They hear a muffled "Switch! Hero Excalibur!" and a golden blade is driven across its stomach; the dragon then falls limp to the ground. The dragon was defeated.

"Javi!" the group yelled.

They rushed towards the dragon's corpse. Javi crawled out

from the dragon's guts. They stopped and were disgusted . Gile realized the gun was in heal mode. He shot Javier. Javier opened his eyes.

"How do you feel?" Gile asked.

Javier, deeply breathing, said, "I hate dragons!"

The group started laughing. Javier got up. He used spatial magic to hold onto the dragon. He used the teleport spell again and brought everyone back. The Party was walking towards the portal. Elly and Lily saw Javi covered in blood. They rushed towards him.

"What happened?" Elly said.

Lily and Elly were worried.

"I told you we'll take care of it," Javier says with an annoyed look.

Javier approaches the resort owner. The owner praises the party.

"Thank you heroes! You're our savior! How could we ever repay you?" the owner said.

"Well, the tickets were pretty expensive," Javier said.

"Of course, we'll give you a 50% discount," the owner said.

"You're out of your mind! We fought a goddamn dragon! It swallowed me alive! I'm covered in its blood and guts! Make it 100% or you'll wish it was the dragon that destroys this place!" Javier said.

'Uh, yes of course!" The owner said in fear.

"Now if you excuse me, I have dragon guts to wash off," Javier said.

Javier was getting praise and thanks from other residents on his way into the resort.

Leo decided to go to sleep. Gile finally found ladies to accompany him in the mixed bath. The girls went back to their bath and Maya explained what happened. Javier was alone in the bath.

A staff member showed up and gave Javier a complimentary beer. Javier took a sip and the staff member left. It's been a while since Javier had alcohol. He looks at the sky, relaxing in the bath. He then gets a flashback of the time he went to a hot spring with his wife and daughter. Javier feels a tear roll down his face.

"Huh?" Javier was confused.

He started tearing up more.

"Damn it," he says.

Javier thought he was going to die as soon as the dragon swallowed him. He downed the beer he was given. Later that night everyone went to bed. Javier couldn't sleep. He got up, put on a bathrobe and walked out. He ran into Maya.

"Javi?" Maya said.

"Why are you up? Javier asked.

"I couldn't sleep," she responded.

"Me either. I was going to just sit in the bath for a bit," Javier said.

"Mind if I join you?" Maya asked.

"Sure," Javier said.

Maya was surprised he agreed. They went to the mixed bath. Maya was a little embarrassed so she wrapped a towel around her body. They sat in the mixed bath in silence for a bit.

"So, that dragon fight was quite intense," Maya said,

"Yeah, I thought it was over when that dragon swallowed me," Javier said.

"Are you feeling okay?"

Javier sighs "Honestly, I'm not sure. It's only been a month and a half since I became the Hero and I had too many close calls. Reminds me of my past," Javier said.

"How so?" Maya asked.

Javier thought for a moment.

"It's a long story," Javier said.

"I don't mind," Maya said.

Javier then explained his back story like he did with Elly on their way to the Royal Capital from the gang life to his family's death and to the point they're at now. Maya learned so much about Javier.

"Wow, that was a lot. You've been through so much," Maya said.

"Yeah well, that's my life I guess. Anyway, enough about my sad upbringing. What about you? I don't know too much about you. First off. What's with the sharpened wand?" Javier asked.

Javier and Maya had a conversation similar to the conversation Maya had with Elly. Javier and Maya started getting more comfortable together. They talked a bit more about her past.

"Damn, you've been through quite a bit yourself," Javier said.

"Yes well, that's the Hero's party for you."

Maya and Javier laugh.

"I do have a question though," Maya said.

"What's up?" Javier said.

"What's your relationship with Elly?" Maya asked.

"We're friends. She was one of the first people I met when I came to this world. She was the very first person I came to trust," Javier responded.

Maya nodded.

"This water feels so nice. The view is also great. It feels romantic," Maya said.

"Well you did insist on sharing this bath with me, you must make the scenery beautiful," Javier said jokingly.

They both laugh. Maya was slightly red in the face.

"May I be honest with you?" Maya asked nervously.

"I would prefer that you be honest with me," Javier said.

"When you made the deal with Lily and you succeeded, I really thought you were going to die. I couldn't bear the thought. I had the same feeling when the dragon swallowed you. There was a tightness in my chest. I concluded that I care for you," Maya said.

"Is that so? I sort of care for you too. All of you. I'm still trying to learn about you guys and am close to completely trusting all of you," Javier responded.

"Close? Is there anyone you're suspicious about?" Maya asked.

"In the beginning, I would have said Leo. After we were arrested together, we had a bit of an understanding of each other. I care for Lily, being a demon shocked me but she's just a kid. I'm going to watch over her. Gile, he seems a little too trusting but he's also simple. He questions when I do something risky which you need but I'll still ignore him sometimes. He doesn't seem like a bad guy though. Elly, I trust her completely. She knows everything about me. Except for the deal with a demon, that's still between us. She'd be so pissed if she found out," Javier said.

"What about me?" Maya asked.

"You? Hmm."

Javier thought for a second.

"I trust you. There's a connection between us that I don't have with the others. I remember when we first met, you tried to seduce me so I wouldn't punch you."

They had a small laugh.

"Yet you still did hit me."

"Yeah, I did."

Javier leans into her ear.

He whispers, "Am I still not hero-like to you?"

She laughs but two inches away from his face. They stared for a second.

Maya leaned in and kissed Javier. They kiss for a few seconds until Javier pulls back slightly .

"Umm..." Javier said, confused.

"Oh my goodness, I am so sorry. I was lost in the moment," Maya said.

"No, that was my fault. I..."

"I'm feeling tired. I'm going to my room. Good night, Javi," Maya said.

She quickly got up and started walking away.

“Maya wait!” Javier said.

She turned and saw Javier looking away, holding her towel. She quickly grabbed the towel and ran to the dressing room. She turned very red.

“Oh my god, I can’t believe that happened,” she thought while touching her lips.

Javier is dumbfounded. He doesn’t know what to feel. Javier sighs.

“Not bad. Damn it,” Javier said.

They eventually all went to sleep and enjoyed the rest of their time at the resort.

CHAPTER 15:
Meeting Demons

After the vacation weekend, the party started taking more quests. They sold the dragon and made 100,000 marbs. As for those curious about the kiss between Javier and Maya, they agreed to pretend that it never happened. They recently took a quest a week later of adventuring through an abandoned dungeon. They were off with Lily staying behind with Elly.

"What are we exactly looking for?" Javier asked.

"The quest just asked to search the dungeon and see if anything seems off. The dungeon was abandoned. Legend says those who enter don't return," Gile said.

"Legends don't mean much in such matters," Leo said.

Javier feels slightly insulted.

Maya is using her fire magic to create a source of light. They have searched for a while and haven't found anything. They come to a stop. There was a two way path.

"Do you think we should split up?" Gile asked.

"We could. I'll go right with Leo. You and Maya go left," Javier said.

"Sounds fair," Maya said, not making eye contact.

"I'll cooperate but try not to drag me into your wild ideas," Leo said.

Javier chuckles. That made Leo a bit uneasy.

"If any seems off, don't face it unless you have to," Javier said.

"Right!" said the group.

The group splits up, with both Maya and Javier leading the way with fire magic as the light source. Javier and Leo run into monsters, but nothing they can't handle. Javier finds a stick, and decides to make a torch with it.

"So far, nothing out of the ordinary," Leo said.

They kept walking and suddenly a step lowered. Javier quickly rolled forward as Leo stepped back. The ceiling caved in.

"Leo, can you hear me? Are you alright?" Javier asked.

"Yes. I'm fine, what about you?" Leo asked.

"I'm good."

"There doesn't seem to be a way in. I'm going to slash through!" Leo suggested.

"Wait, don't! The torch landed on your side, go down Maya and Gile's path," Javier said.

"What? Why?" Leo questioned.

"You said not to drag you into my wild ideas. Trust me, I'll be fine. I have an idea!" Javier said.

"Don't make me regret this!" Leo said as he took the torch and ran back to catch up to Maya and Gile.

Javi twists his ring to Level 1. "Night Vision!" Javier chanted. Demons have the ability to see better in the dark but not humans so he's using light magic to boost his vision along with his demon abilities. As Javier moves along, he raises the level on his ring. Javier suddenly stops. There is no more floor. He looks down and sees a light. He gets flashbacks.

"Please just stop being reckless," Aisha said.

"Stay out of trouble," Elly said.

"Don't make me regret this!" Leo said.

Javier stood there for a second. Javier sighed and raised his ring to Level 3. He then jumped. He used air magic to land lightly. He looks around. It's a room full of demons. They all look at Javier in confusion. Part of the floor rises and grabs Javier's left arm. It pulled him against the wall. The wall latched his other arm. Two demons approach Javier. Both are female.

"Who are you?" Asked the demon on his left.

"Javier..." he said.

"You're human but also, a demon?" the same demon said.

"Additionally, I think it would be a good idea to introduce yourself."

The same demon is annoyed at his comment. The other demon held her back.

"I'm the Demon General, Nino," said the demon on his right.

"Saki," said the demon on his left with her arms crossed.

"Alright, Nino and Saki. Think you can release me before I cause chaos?"

"Oh you think a mere human can do so?" Saki said.

"Well for starters, I'm half demon. I think we just skipped past that. Secondly I'm not just some human," Javier said.

Saki is getting more irritated by Javier's attitude.

"Saki," Nino said as she snapped her finger.

Saki sucks her teeth and lets Javier go.

"Alright, Nino was it? I appreciate that," Javier said, sticking out his hand.

Nino knocks away his hand.

"What business do you have here?" Nino asked.

"Well, I'm on a quest. This dungeon was supposedly abandoned but doesn't seem so from the looks of it. There were also rumors that if someone were to enter the dungeon, they wouldn't come back out," Javier responded.

"Correct," Nino said, looking left.

Javier looks and sees skeletons in a pile of past adventurers.

"I see, why?" He asks.

"Humans are not allowed to discover this place," Saki said.

"Well I'm half demon. So we're cool?" Javier said.

"What is your deal?" Saki said annoyed.

"What's your deal?" Javier said back.

"That's it!" Saki yelled, running at Javier.

She swung and Javier ducked and swept her feet. She landed on her back.

"She swung on me," Javier said.

"Enough playing around Saki," Nino said.

"What is this place anyway? Secret war meeting? I thought it wasn't for another ten months or so?" Javier said.

The demons look at Javier in shock that he knows that.

The demon's guards are up.

"How do you know such a thing?" Nino asks.

"A goddess told me," he responded.

"Goddess? He's the Hero!" Nino said.

The demons ready their weapons.

"Whoa, whoa, that's a bit much don't you think?" Javier asked.

"Silence! Your opinion here does not matter!" Nino said more sternly.

"Well, for someone who doesn't care for my opinion, I think you could have dressed more conservatively," Javier said.

Nino is getting annoyed.

"How dare you speak bitterly of our general?" Saki asked.

"I mean. I didn't mean it like that. I think she's attractive but showing a bit too much skin, in my opinion," he responded mockingly.

Nino is embarrassed and irritated.

Javier turns down his ring all the way. He is now a whole human.

Saki uses her earth magic again to grab both of Javier's arms.

"Enough of your jokes, Hero. Attack!" Nino says.

"Fine, have it your way," Javier said.

Javier broke out of the earth's magic easily. Saki is shocked. Demons rush in. Javier is knocking them out. Javier suddenly gets grabbed by an earth golem. It's holding him up from behind.

"Try to fight back now!" Saki said.

Javier tucks his head down and inhales deeply. He rams the back of his head into the golem, shattering it. Saki was surprised. He pulls out his knife and starts slashing demons.

Javier's power was too much for the ordinary demons. Nino and Saki were the only two left. They look at each other and attack simultaneously. Javier dodges and stops both of their punches, holding them. He looks at Nino and winks. Nino grits her teeth. Saki lands a scratch on Javier's chest and Nino punches him across the room.

Javier is coughing.

"Holy shit, you're strong," Javier said.

He kneels. "Summon Lion," Javier chanted.

An all-black lion formed and attacked Saki, but Saki killed it in one punch.

"Really?" Saki asked, not impressed.

The ground suddenly sinks and tightens around Nino and Saki's shoulder level. They were shocked because he didn't chant anything.

"He's a Non-Chanter?" Saki asked.

"No, Multi-Caster," Javier said.

He walks up to the demons.

"Now then. What to do?" Javier said.

"Wait!" Nino yelled.

"You win. We surrender." Nino said.

Javier kneels and asks "Do you think I'm stupid or something?"

"Well," Saki said.

Javier chuckles and then sinks her more into the ground at chin level. He raises Nino out of the hole and tightens it on Saki.

"Why just her?" Saki says.

Javier ignores her.

"Look, my quest was to search the dungeon and see if anything was off. I'm not looking to fight you anymore. At least not yet. Don't worry, I won't tell anyone," Javier said.

Nino looks confused.

"What is this trickery? I don't believe you," Nino asks.

"No tricks, just give the Demon Lord this message." Javier said, walking towards the wall.

"See you in ten months. I'm the last person that you'll see before I kill you!" Javier says menacingly and glares.

Nino was a bit taken aback.

"Don't mess with me!" Nino yells while charging Javier with a winded up fist.

Javier quickly turns with his hands out and Nino's punch hits the wall beside his head. Javier is accidentally holding her breasts. Nino is in utter shock.

"Shit. Okay, two things before you kill me. First off, this was a complete accident. Secondly, not bad," Javier says as he nods in satisfaction.

Nino starts growling out of pure hatred.

"Too far?" he asked sarcastically.

Nino swings at Javier repeatedly. He keeps dodging and punches Nino in the gut. Nino goes down.

"Sorry, I have to go. Be sure to deliver that message." Javier said.

"What about me?" Saki said

Javier looked at her and rolled his eyes.

He uses earth magic to rise to the path he was in prior.

He shuts the pathway and Saki is launched out at the exact moment the risen ground slams back down. Saki gets back up and runs towards Nino.

"Are you okay, General?" Saki asks.

Nino coughs, "Next time I see that Hero, I'm going to kill him."

Javier uses spatial magic to exit the dungeon's entryway where the rest of the group are.

"Javi!" Gile and Maya say.

"Did you find anything?" Javier asked.

"No, it was a dead end," Gile said.

"Same for me. Just monsters," Javier said.

The group goes back to the guild and reports that there was nothing. Javier mentioned to them that the dungeon is useless and to close it off; it's just a monster-infested tunnel. The guild takes his word for it and decides to close off the dungeon.

Nino and Saki are in front of the Demon Lord kneeling.

"I heard that you had an unexpected guest," The Demon Lord said.

"Yes, well, it was the Hero," Nino responded.

Kaval seemed intrigued.

"He had a message for you," Saki mentioned. Kaval signaled her to deliver.

"See you in ten months. I'm the last person that you'll see before I kill you!" Saki said.

"I see. This Hero is like no other. He truly is interesting," Kaval says as he laughs.

CHAPTER 16:
Royal Escort

The King requested Javier to meet at the castle. He and Elly head over to the castle. They enter and are greeted by guards, Harry and the King.

"Hero," Harry says.

"Mini, yes man," Javier responds.

"I see your attitude hasn't changed," Harry says.

"Neither has your height," Javier responded.

"Alright, that's enough Javi," Elly said.

"Thank you, Elly. Always a pleasure," the King says.

Elly bows.

"So what's with the sudden request?" Javier asked.

"I need you to escort my son to a neighboring town to and from," the King says.

"No." Javier says.

"I wasn't asking," says the King.

"I'm not doing it," Javier responded.

"Alright, name your price," the King said.

"Why do you want me specifically to do it?" Javier asked.

"You've seemed to be the strongest of them all and protecting royalty seems fitting for you," the King says.

"Fine, and as for the price," Javier said.

The King sighs. "What is it?"

"100 platinum coins."

"Alright," the King says.

"And?" Javier said.

"And?" the King asked.

"Harry has to kneel to me right here," Javier says, pointing to yard away from his standing position.

"What? How despicable!" Harry says.

"Fine," the King says.

Harry looks at the king in utter shock.

"He named his price. It's for my son," the King says.

Harry meets Javier from a yard away and kneels with despair.

"Sickening waste of a Hero," Harry mumbled.

"Sorry I couldn't hear you from down there," Javier said grinning.

Harry grits his teeth.

"Okay, I'll do it." Javier said satisfied.

"Yes, I will schedule a carriage for tomorrow morning," the King says.

The following day, Javier meets with the carriage driver and Prince Lance.

"I appreciate you looking after me, Hero," Lance says as he bows.

"Sure," Javier said.

Javier and Lance enter the carriage and are now on their way. There was an awkward silence for a while. They had never interacted before.

"So, any plan on defeating the Demon Lord?" Lance asks.

"Not really," Javier said.

"Huh?" Lance asked, shocked.

"Yeah, I still have around nine months left," Javier responded.

"I would strongly recommend you come up with a plan sooner than later."

"No thanks."

"I honestly don't understand why you were hired."

"Big talk from a spoiled rich kid."

"I'm not spoiled."

"You're a prince that your dad hired, the Hero to guard you on this journey."

"That was my father."

"He pisses me off," Javier said.

Lance chuckles.

"What's so funny?" Javier asked.

"I never heard someone openly talk about my father like that more than you," Lance says.

"Well yeah. I call him King Hassle."

Lance starts laughing.

"Clever," Lance says.

"You like that? How about this? As part of my payment, I had Harry kneel to me."

"No way," Lance said.

"He did," Javier said proudly.

Lance and Javier laugh.

"You're not so bad Lance. You don't irritate me like your father," Javier said.

Lance looks at Javier shocked.

"What's up?" Javier questioned.

"No one has ever called me just Lance before. It's always 'Your Majesty' or 'Prince'," Lance says.

"I couldn't care less about your status," Javier says.

"I see."

"Sounds like your father shelters you and your status affects how people talk to you."

"No, he does that exactly. I wish that sometimes I could be a normal person and not be 'The Prince' sometimes."

"What if I said you can?" Javier asks.

"What do you mean?" Lance asks.

"I can use light magic to change your hair and eye color. The meeting is tomorrow. No one would recognize you if we went out tonight."

"Really? That would be fantastic. But they would never allow it."

"I'm your guard, I'm sure you don't have to worry."

"He has a separate guard for my room."

Javier sighs.

"Okay, I have a plan but you'll have to break quite a bit of rules. Are you in?"

Lance thinks for a bit.

"I'm in."

They fist bump. Later that night, Javier used a portal in Lance's room and snuck him out. Javier changed their hair and eye color.

"I can't believe it," Lance said excitedly.

"Alright, what do you want to do?" Javier asks.

"I'm not sure. I never had this freedom before," Lance says.

"Alright, I have an idea, but it will be breaking more rules."

"Let's do it," Lance says.

They walk through an ally.

There are two men standing there, talking suspiciously.

"Hey, you guys know where we can make quick cash?" Javier says.

The two men get suspicious of Javier and Lance.

"Easy now, I'm not undercover. Here's for your troubles," Javier said as he handed them two gold coins.

The two men lowered their guards.

"Yeah, we know a place. Continue down and turn right. First door on your right," one of the guys said.

Javier and Lance go where they pointed. They go down the staircase of the building. There is a crowd and, in the middle, two men are fighting. People are placing bets.

"Lance, got any cash on you?" Javier asks.

Lance shows his cash. Javier quickly covers it.

"Watch it. You're going to get robbed holding that much in this area," Javier said.

Javier grabs a Platinum coin. Lance puts the rest away.

"Okay, when you see me enter the circle, say 'I got platinum on hood'."

"Alright?" Lance said, confused.

Javier puts on his hood, and enters the circle.

"I got platinum on the hood," Lance said.

"No way."

"Not a chance."

"Big bucks here."

The settler takes his bet.

Javier's opponent is big.

Lance is getting worried.

Javier pulls down his hood.

"Ready! Fight!" says the ref.

Javier dodges the guy's swing and elbows him. He followed with three quick jabs to the guy's ribs. He then spin kicks the guy. The guy goes down and won't get up. He gets dragged away. The crowd goes wild, including Lance. Lance was the only one to bet on Javier. He won triple what he bet.

"Are you making another bet?" the settler asks Lance.

A guy on watch runs in.

"Shut it down! Guards are coming!" he yells.

Everyone starts running out of the building. Guards are chasing people. Javier runs to Lance, grabs his arm and pulls him.

"Follow me! Try to keep up," Javier said.

Lance follows.

Javier and Lance have a guard closing in on them. They run down an alleyway that's a dead end.

"What do we do?" Lance asks.

"We jump the wall," Javier says.

Javier kicks off the wall on his right, over the wall. He looks back waiting for Lance. Lance jumps over the wall completely.

"Nice! Let's go," Javier said. They make the distance between them and the guards wider. Javier puts his hood away with his spatial magic. He pulls out a regular shirt.

"Here, put this on. They won't notice you if we run into the guards," Javier says.

Lance changes his shirt.

"That was incredible!" Lance said.

"Alright let's grab some food and drinks. You're old enough right?"

"Yes but I never had it."

"Oh man, you're in for a treat," Javier says.

They go to a local pub and order food and drinks. They cheered and drank. A girl was checking out Lance.

"Hey, that girl is checking you out," Javier said.

Lance seems embarrassed.

"Go talk to her," Javier pressured.

"What do I say?" Lance asked nervously.

"Just be confident, and don't blow your cover."

Lance takes a quick sip of beer and walks up to the girl. They chat for a bit and Lance eventually comes back with the girl's info.

"Okay, smooth talker. Nice going," Javier said.

"That was nerve-wracking," Lance said.

"Alright, let's head back before they find out you're gone," Javier suggested.

"Thanks a lot Javier. Tonight was so much fun," Lance said.

"No problem. Let me know if you want to do something like this again. It's been a while since I've gone out drinking," Javier said.

Javier and Lance teleport back to their rooms.

Javier puts a recovery spell on Lance.

"What are you doing?" Lance asks.

"I'll get in trouble if I let you go to the meeting with a hangover." Javier said.

The next day they completed their meeting and went back home.

Prince Lance is having a conversation with the King.

"Are you alright? Did the hero do anything?" the King asked.

"The Hero completed his job. He didn't do anything wrong," Lance said.

CHAPTER 17:
Party Picnic

The group is eating breakfast. Lily has an important question to ask everyone at the table.

"Can we go on a picnic?" Lily asks.

Javier looks at her for a bit.

"Sure," Javier said.

"That sounds fun," Elly said.

"Don't you guys ever tell her no?" Leo says.

"You don't want to have a picnic?" Lily asked with sad eyes.

Leo turns, "Alright," he says as he adjusts his glasses.

"You were saying?" Javier teased.

"Oh shut up," Leo said.

Gile and Maya also agree. Lily gets excited. They pack things and use Javier's spatial magic to carry everything. They head over to a flower field where there are few monsters ever spotted. They unload everything and sit down.

Javier brought a ball. Javier kicks it to Lily.

"Have you ever played soccer Lily?" Javier asked.

"Soccer?" Lily asked, confused.

"It's a sport where you play in teams and kick a ball into your opponent's net."

"I want to try!" Lily said excitedly.

"Leo, you and Gile are a team," Javier said.

"I'm not interested," Leo said.

"You're right, you probably couldn't beat me anyway."

"Is that so? I'll show you," Leo said.

"Too easy," Javier thought.

Javier makes two goalposts out of rock and nets out of vines using earth magic. Javier kneels, "Summon Shadow Clones," he chants. Two shadow humans appear.

"Alright you guys are playing goalie. Stand in front of a goal each and block the ball from going in. Got it?" Javier said to the clones.

They give a thumbs up. They are at their goals.

"Alright, no hands allowed except for the goalie. Only use your feet. Additionally, there is no fighting or physical contact. Ready?" Javier asks.

"Ready!" Lily and Gile said.

Javier passes to Lily. Lily runs up the field. Gile is in the way. Lily kicks towards Leo's direction. Leo runs ahead and kicks the ball towards the goal but the goalie blocks it. Javier gets the ball and runs up the field. He dribbles past Leo and Gile. He kicks and scores. He and Lily celebrate.

"Alright, your ball," Javier says.

Leo passes to Gile. Gile runs up and gets past Lily. He passes across the field to Leo. Leo shoots and scores. Leo and

Gile celebrate. Javier walks up to his goalie.

"What was that? You could have blocked that. You call that defense?" Javier says to the goalie.

Javier's goalie pushes him. Javier punches his Shadow Clone.

"This is what we're doing?" Javier said.

The goalie disappears. Javier kneels and summons another clone.

"Okay, it's becoming too much. Next goal wins," Javier said,

Javier passes to Lily. She runs up the field. She dribbles past Gile. She passes the ball to Javier. He dribbles past Leo and Leo trips. Javier passes to Lily and Lily shoots. She scores. Elly and Maya cheer for Lily.

"GOOOOOOOOOOOOOOAL!" Javier yells.

"Okay, good game," Gile said.

"Lucky win," Leo says.

"Sore loser," Javier said teasingly.

The group laughs.

"Elly, let's play," Lily says.

"I don't know. That game seems too much for me." Elly said.

"Don't worry, I made this," Javier says, holding a handmade kite.

"What is it?" Lily asks.

"It's called a kite. Watch, hold this ball of yarn," Javier says.

Javier walks a small distance with the kite.

"Okay, now run to Elly," Javier said.

Lily runs towards Elly and the kite lifts a little bit. Javier uses wind magic to make it go higher. The kite is in the air.

"Wow! Look Elly!" Lily says excitedly.

"Now run around for a bit," Javier said.

Lily and Elly play with the kite for a while. The rest of the group was chatting and making jokes.

Everyone is getting hungry so they open the picnic basket.

Everyone grabs a sandwich. They all enjoy the sandwiches.

"Oh wow, this is good. Elly you made this?" Javier said.

Elly blushes. Maya notices.

"Javi, I brought this rare wine. You have to try it," Maya says.

Javier gets a glass and Maya pours him some of the wine. Javier sips it.

"I'm not a wine person, but that's actually pretty good. Thanks for bringing this," Javier said.

Maya blushes. Elly notices.

"Javi, would you like another sandwich?" Elly asks.

"Sure," Javier says.

"How about more wine?" Maya asks.

"Alright?" Javier questions.

"What are they doing?" Lily asks Leo.

Leo adjusts his glasses, "That is a battle between women fighting over Javier's attention. It's best not to interfere," he says.

"Why does he get all the attention?" Gile thought.

"Javi, do you want some fruit?" Lily asks.

Javier takes some of her fruit and takes a bite.

"That is the best. Thank you, Lily," Javier says with a big smile.

Maya and Elly feel defeated.

"I'm not sure why they're competing, but I will go with Lily every time," Javier thought.

Javier feels sleepy so he decides to take a nap. He opens his eyes and of course, he is having a meeting with Aisha. Javier opens his eyes and sees Aisha has her arms crossed looking away.

Javier sighs, "What is it? I didn't do anything this time." Javier said.

"Looks like you're having fun. Picnics, Hot Springs, romantic rivalry. You haven't thought about talking to me for a long time," Aisha says with jealousy.

"Goddess," Javier said.

"Hmph," Aisha says.

"Aisha," Javier said.

Aisha smiles and chuckles a bit.

"Okay, I wanted to ask you something. It's about your interaction with the Demon General," Aisha said.

"That was a complete accident," Javier said.

"That's not what I'm talking about. I would much rather talk about that instead. You were being quite the womanizer lately."

"How?"

"You want me to point it out? Let's start with right now. Elly and Maya are fighting over your attention."

"They weren't doing that. I was enjoying my lunch."

"How about when you kissed Maya."

"Okay, first of all, Maya kissed me. Secondly, we both agreed, that never happened."

"It didn't seem like it to me."

"None of them were me taking the initiative."

"Oh really? What about the Demon General? Feeling her boobs isn't taking the initiative? Not to mention you told her they were nice?"

Javier stayed quiet.

"What would your wife think?" Aisha asked.

"Didn't you have a question about the Demon General?" Javier asked.

"I was only going to ask why you chose not to kill the two lead demons and kept it secret from the guild and party. Teasing you seemed more fun," Aisha said.

Javier sighs.

"I thought I would have to wait for the war to start. Plus, if I did, I think the war would start prematurely and I would've technically started it. Plus, leaving that annoying demon in the ground and having her thinking I was going to leave her in there was very satisfying," Javier said.

Aisha sighs but already knows that's how Javier does things.

"One more thing, the dragon. Was being swallowed part of the plan?" Aisha asked.

"Okay, we're done here," Javier said.

"Fine, time to wake up Hero. Until we meet again," Aisha said.

Javier woke up in reality.

Everyone is exhausted. Lily is already asleep in Elly's lap.

"Alright, the picnic is over. Let's go home," Javier said.

Javier uses his magic to pick up and makes a portal to the guild. Everyone goes home and sleeps except for Javier. Javier decides to go to the quest board. He sees a familiar face.

"Hey, Lila," Javier says.

"Oh, Javier! I didn't know you were coming today," Lila said nervously, fixing her hair.

"Right, I was just wondering if you had any small quests I could do?"

"Of course. Give me one second," Lila says, shuffling through quests.

Lila hands over a quest about a suspicion of smuggling in the Royal Capital.

"Hmm, okay. Seems easy enough," Javier says.

"There is one slight problem. It's in the Red District, meaning there are a lot of sex workers," Lila says.

"You were being quite the womanizer lately," Javier remembers Aisha tells him.

"On second thought, I think I'm going to rest for the day. Thank you though."

"R-Right, not a problem," Lila said.

CHAPTER 18:
Elly Is Missing

Everyone is having breakfast however, Elly isn't there. Everyone is wondering where Elly is. Javier went to Elly's room and she wasn't there. He then went to the guild's front counter to ask if anyone had seen Elly. Lila was at the front desk.

"Lila, I'm glad I ran into you," Javier said.

"R-Really?" Lila asked, surprised.

"Yeah, have you seen Elly? We can't seem to find her," Javier asked.

"Oh, no, I haven't seen her since yesterday. Though this weird man was talking to her yesterday," Lila said.

"Weird man? What happened?"

"Well, he was being a creep talking about how he would love to take her home and tie her up," Lila said.

"What does he look like?"

"He had blonde hair. He was around six feet tall. He had a bit of hair on his chin but not a full beard. He was wearing a purple suit with white stripes. He had yellow sunglasses. He also had a fedora with a feather on it."

"Okay, I'm not certain but this guy might have kidnapped Elly. I'm going to find out," Javier said.

"What are you going to do when you find out?" Lila asked.

"I don't know. I guess we'll find out," Javier said.

Javier tells the group about the description of the guy. They searched all over town and did not see the guy. Leo then found someone who fit the description. He followed him to his home. He noticed that his bookshelf had a book missing in the center. Later he saw that there was a book filling that space; the guy was nowhere to be found in the house. Javier decides that they're going to ambush his house. Later that night they saw the man leave his house. They snuck into the man's house. They found the book on the man's table top. Javier hesitates.

"What's wrong Javi?" Maya asks.

"This seems a little too easy. The man happens to leave his home when we're near and leaves his book in plain sight? He was wearing what he was wearing yesterday? Gile, you and Leo check out the secret passage. Lily, stay close between me and Maya," Javier said.

"Boss! You're going to want to see this!" Gile yelled.

Javier went into the passage along with Maya and Lily which led to a staircase. He went down the stairs and saw a long hall of cells. There were girls chained up in the cells. They were terrified and covered in injuries. Maya covered Lily's eyes.

"What the hell?" Javier said.

"You know it's not nice breaking into people's houses, Hero," the man in the purple suit said from a distance.

Everyone turned and the man released gas from his hands. He used it as a smoke screen. Javier with limited sight did see a group of men in all black rush in. He then was knocked out. He woke up minutes later as well as Maya, Gile, and Leo. Lily was gone. Javier looked around in a panic. He's getting flashbacks of his family dying.

"No, No, No, No!" Javier yelled.

Maya grabbed his hands. "Javi, look at me. Look at me!" she yelled.

Javier is looking at her.

"We're going to find them but you cannot panic. You need to concentrate," she says. Javier is hyperventilating but is trying to calm down.

"Okay, okay," He said.

He started grasping his sanity little by little.

"Gile, break open the cells. Leo, cut the chains. Maya, undo the locks on their collars," Javier said calmly.

Javier pulls out a bag full of platinum coins. An estimate of 500,000 Marbs. He opens a portal to the guild.

Javier is face-to-face with these girls. He sees them beaten and battered. He takes out his gun. He chants "Switch!" into a shotgun. Leo is surprised. Javier casts heal on it. He then heals the girls.

"BANG" "BANG" "BANG" "BANG" "BANG"

"Gile, Leo, take these girls to the guild. Give this bag to the guild. Get these girls help and rooms. We'll meet you later at the guild. Maya and I have to make a stop where we might get a clue," Javier said.

The girls were escorted to the guild and found a psychiatrist for the girls.

Javier and Maya went to Doctor Fern's shop.

A customer is trying to heckle Fern.

"25 Marbs."

"For the last time, it's 50 Marbs! Take it or leave it!" Fern said.

"Oh look at that, it's free. Get out now!" Maya rushes the customer out.

Javier drops two silver coins for the item on the counter.

Maya closes up the shop. She then takes Javier and Fern to the back room.

"What is going on? Why is he looking panicked?" Fern asked.

"Look, the demon girl was kidnapped as well as our elf friend," Maya explained.

Javier looks Fern in the eyes.

"Does my deal have something that can tell me where Lily is?" Javier asked.

"I don't know for a fact. Let me check my notes," Fern says.

Fern is reviewing his notes on demon deal research.

"Alright, here. If you concentrate your mana on your demon hand and place her DNA on it. Your mind can open up a path to where she is."

Javier shifts his ring. Level 1, Level 2, and now Level 3. Javier checks his hood for Lily's hair. Maya sees one and pulls it out. He concentrates his mana and places Lily's hair. Javier closes his eyes. He sees a path leading to Lily and sees Lily chained up.

"Get me a map!" Javier yells.

Fern grabs him a map of the Royal Capital and a pen. Javier redraws the path to Lily and circles an abandoned factory.

Javier turns down his ring's level.

They meet up with Leo and Gile at the guild. They leave without explaining much and end up at the factory in moments. They stop at the entrance. Javier is getting flashbacks of when he entered the abandoned warehouse. How he lost his life.

Maya grabs Javier's face and gets close to him, forcing him to see her.

"We're going to save them," Maya says.

Javier snaps back to reality for a brief moment.

"Let's do this!" Javier said.

"Right!" the others say.

The group then rams through the entrance to be welcomed by Men in Black and the Man in the Suit.

"Well, well, if it ain't the Hero with his group. Oh wait, you seem to be missing some people," the man says.

Javier grits his teeth.

"Maya, I'm going to have to use it," Javier says.

Leo and Gile are confused.

"Leo, Gile, I'm sorry," Javier said.

"Javi, Wait!" Maya said.

Javier slowly switched his ring level up.

"CLICK" "CLICK" "CLICK."

Black and white hair, crimson red eye, his left hand is a

demon claw. There was an addition to his transformation. The left side of his back grew a demon wing. Javier flaps it.

Everyone but Maya was shocked.

"Hold on, they never said this in his description of their abilities," the man in a suit said.

Javier glides and is in the face of the suited man in less than a second. The man didn't have any time to process that speed, let alone react. Javier grabs his throat and tackles him through the wall. He punches the man in the face with his left hand using his demon strength which is amplified by his Hero strength. The man is dead in one punch. Maya strikes one of the men in all black. Gile comes to his senses and attacks as well. Leo is still in shock. The men in all black were taken out. Javier places Lily's hair in his demon hand. He locates her underneath the factory. He finds the hidden trapdoor. He jumps down the steps and the hall he sees a man he hasn't seen before, Elly chained up, and Lily chained up.

Maya, Gile, and Leo catch up to Javier.

The man is holding knives up to both Elly and Lily's throats.

"Now, I believe that you wouldn't want anything to happen to them so this is what we're going to do. You're going to walk back up those steps, I'll put down these knives, and I'll pleasure myself to my heart's content, and then I'm going to sell them for a handsome amount of money to slave traders," the man says and laughs. Javier walks out. Maya, Gile, and Leo watch Javier walk out.

The man laughs again and says "I see the Hero is too far

gone to put up a fight!"

A transportation portal opens up behind the man. A demon claw reaches over and has a hold of the man's cranium as his arms are sliced off in an instant. The man was then pulled through the portal and the portal closed. Javier, minutes later, walked back down the stairs in his standard form as if nothing happened. He breaks the lock on Elly and Lily. He pulls out his gun and casts his heal on it.

"BANG" "BANG"

Both Elly and Lily are unconscious. Javier teleports to Elly's room and drops them off. He teleports back. Javier takes a deep breath. He turns around to see Leo in his face holding a sword up to Javier's throat.

"Please tell me that I didn't see what I saw," Leo yelled in a sorrowful voice.

"Leo." Javier said.

"Did you make me open up about my past for your own gain? Leo yelled.

"No."

"Did you make up the story about your family being murdered to seem sympathetic?"

"No–."

"You're a disgraceful waste of a Hero. Is there anything else you were hiding from us?" Leo asked.

"The demon I made a deal with is Lily," Javier said in a defeated voice.

Gile is shocked and Leo is at a loss for words. Leo looks at

Maya.

"Did you know? You don't seem even a bit surprised," Leo questioned.

"I knew. I'm sorry," Maya said.

"Maya?" Gile said.

"Does Elly know?" Gile asked.

"Elly knows Lily is a demon. Not about my deal," Javier said.

Leo lets go and walks out.

"Leo, wait!" Javier said as Maya cut him off.

"Let him go, he'll need time before you try to talk to him," Maya said.

"Gile?" Javier said.

"Honestly this is a lot to take in all at once. Let's get some rest and talk about it tomorrow. For now I'm heading home," Gile said.

"Do you want to teleport there?" Javier asked.

"Um, no it's okay. I could use a walk alone right now. I'll see you tomorrow," Gile said.

CHAPTER 19:
Where Our Trust Lies

Javier and Maya teleport to Javier's room. Maya sits on Javier's bed and calls Javier to come to the bed. Javier lays on his bed, mentally exhausted. Maya lies next to Javier.

"Maya, what should I do?" Javier asks.

Maya takes a deep breath. "I don't know. We're in this together. You put your trust in me with everything. I can do nothing but the same. I'm with you until the end," Maya says.

"That means a lot, truly," Javier said.

"Get some rest, we'll check on Elly and Lily later," Maya said.

Javier falls asleep. He didn't talk to Aisha. He eventually woke up. He saw Maya lying asleep in his bed next to him. He's finally grasping the reality of the situation at hand. He jumps out of bed, waking up Maya and runs to Elly's room. He bursts open her door and sees Elly and Lily awake and in tears because they're glad they are safe and back home. Javier runs up to them and hugs them. Maya catches up to Javier. She stands at the doorway.

"I'm so sorry," Javier said.

"That was so scary," Lily whimpered.

Elly stayed quiet.

"Elly, Lily, we have some things to discuss with you two, eo, and Gile. Meet us in the diner in the morning," Javier says.

Javier rents out the diner for the party to talk in private.

Javier and Maya are sitting at a table. Elly and Lily join them a bit later. Gile arrives shortly after them. They're waiting for Leo. Leo eventually shows up. They're all sitting in silence. There is awkward tension all around them.

"Okay, so Gile and Leo already know everything. Elly you knew Lily was a demon. However, I never told you that I made a deal with Lily. In other words, I made a deal with a demon. I'm now officially part demon," Javier said.

Elly paused. "Wow, okay," she said.

"Okay? That's all you have to say?" Leo questioned.

"I'm letting it sit so I can process it," Elly said.

"What I want to know is how I can trust you when you don't trust me with essential information," Gile said.

"Gile, I'm going to say in full confidence that you can trust me. I know that I wasn't frank with you guys at first. I deeply apologize for that, I didn't know what would happen if I did tell you. Now it resulted in you finding out the worst way possible," Javier said.

"I spilled everything to you. I said things that I never told anyone before, and you went and did what caused me the most pain in my life. I don't know how you expect me to forgive you, let alone trust you," Leo said.

"You're right, I'm sorry, truly. I can't take back what I did, but I can promise no more secrets," Javier said.

"I thought hard about this and I'm going to say this now. It was nice having the honor to be part of this party, but as of now, I'm resigning as a member of this party and going my own separate way," Leo said.

"Leo," Javier said.

"Hero, I made my decision. Unfortunately it came to this but the wall of trust we built no longer stands. Elly, it was nice working with you. Gile, I am honored to have had a comrade like you. Maya, I did enjoy working with you though part of the trust we built has fallen also. Lily..." Leo pauses.

Leo grits his teeth. "Best of luck to you and your future endeavors," Leo said.

"I'm still staying as a member of the party, but only during quests and defeating the Demon Lord. I respect you Javi, I do. Maya, the same goes for you. Elly, we haven't interacted that much but I did enjoy working with you," Gile said.

"Gile," Javier said.

"Javi, I want to trust you. I will continue to support you but these things you are doing are putting Lily in danger now. I'm going back to my town for a while and Lila will be in charge of your quests. I also think it's best if I take Lily with me," Elly said.

"What?!" Javier said.

"I'm sorry Javi, my mind is made up. I specialize in light magic so I can hide her identity. We will return, but I'm not certain when," Elly said.

"Elly," Javier said.

"Lily?" Javier asked.

"Javi, a long time ago I heard you and Elly talk about you leaving. What does that mean?" Lily asked.

Javier hesitated.

"Lily, you know how I'm the Hero right?" Javier asks.

Lily nods.

"Well, because I'm the Hero, that also means I'm from another world. In my old world, I had a wife and a daughter. Bad people killed them. If I defeat the Demon Lord then, I get a wish. That means I can go back to my world and live a peaceful life with them again. That means I wouldn't be able to come back," Javier said.

"Oh," Lily said and tears welled up in her eyes.

"Do you have any more questions?" Javier asked Lily.

Lily nods no.

"I don't think I need to speak but I may as well. I'm here with Javier. To the end. I understand the situation is different with me compared to you but, we all have the end goal of defeating the Demon Lord. I don't quite get why it's no longer the main problem. I believe we're missing the big picture. If you want time apart, by all means take it. But I don't see reason not to continue the journey to defeat the Demon Lord," Maya said.

The group went silent.

"I honestly think it's best if we went our separate ways for now," Leo said as he got up and left.

“Let me know if we have any quests,” Gile said as he got up and left.

Elly and Lily get up to pack their things. Javier and Maya follow them up. Javier goes to his room to grab something. Elly and Lily are almost done packing.

Javier hands Elly Lily’s knife.

“Javi,” Elly says.

“Please, just in case. I’ve said it before, I want her to know at least how to defend herself,” Javier said.

Elly takes Lily’s knife. They finished packing.

“Do you want to be teleported there?” Javier asks.

“That would be appreciated,” Elly said.

Javier opens a portal. Javier hugs Elly.

“Take good care of yourself and Lily. I’ll see you later,” Javier said to Elly

“I’ll see you, Javi,” Elly said.

Maya hugged Lily.

“Take of Elly for me alright? Stay strong for her,” Maya said to Lily.

“Right,” Lily said, tears in her eyes.

Maya hugs Elly.

“Take care Elly. I’m going to miss having a friend who isn’t always looking to smash heads,” Maya said.

“I’ll miss you too,” Elly said.

Javier hugs Lily. They hugged for a while.

“I’ll miss you... I love you Lily,” Javier said, fighting tears.

Lily starts crying.

"I-I-I love you too Javi. I'll miss you," Lily said.

Elly and Lily leave through Javier's portal and the portal closes.

Javier is trying to hold in his sorrow. Maya hugs Javier and Javier is near his breaking point.

"It's alright. Let it out. We're in this together," Maya said.

Gile is standing outside the door listening in. He then walks back to his room.

CHAPTER 19.5:
Our Own Paths

It's been a month since the Hero's party parted ways. Everyone is going down their path. Leo moved back in with his family. They keep commenting on how he's a "Failed Noble" from a "Failed Hero's Party." Leo has been taking solo quests. Leo soon became an S-Rank adventurer. He tries not to think about the Hero's Party. The comments he hears from others no longer phase him. Leo has become a well known adventurer among the guild and is known to complete every solo quest perfectly.

Gile only interacts with Javier and Maya when they have a quest to do but doesn't say much. He has taken solo quests as well. Gile is on the market, looking for a girlfriend. He's been on a few dates, but none of them worked out. Gile is either too nervous, or it's because he was part of the Hero's Party that split up. He isn't giving up yet, he keeps looking forward and building his strength and endurance.

Elly and Lily have been doing pretty good so far since they went to Elly's old town. Elly has been taking charge of the guild while the Guild master takes care of out of town business. Elly is living the life she did before she met Javier, but with a few exceptions considering Lily is living with her. Lily has gotten a tutor for magic. It's an old professor that the guild master recommended. She has no political views on race or origin. Lily is gifted in magic and has been working on her academics. Elly decided to have her learn about self defense from an instructor. She's reading a lot and journaling about her day to day life. As far as it goes for them two, they're doing pretty well. They do miss the feeling of not knowing what to expect from Javier but they try their best not to think too much about it knowing it's for the best right now.

As Maya did say, she's there with Javier. They've been doing their regular party quests but they also have been taking duo quests along with solo quests. Most assume that they are in a relationship but they deny all the rumors. They are friends and nothing more they said. They are still very close and seem to be doing pretty well. Javier has been working on himself and learning to look forward to the future. He has been doing better mentally and emotionally as of late and Maya has been by his side the entire time. They lean on each other and depend on each other both on the quests and in their personal lives.

CHAPTER 20: Nomans Village

There have been rumors that there is a village partially on human property that is filled with demons. It's in a small village called "Nomans Village." It's a part of land neither fully claimed by humans nor demons. As the name suggests, no humans live there. It's an abandoned village that used to be for refugees during the war on demons back when the past Hero was battling the past Demon Lord. It's now a refugee village for runaway demons who want no part in the Demon Lord's control or the war the demons will be declaring on humans. There has been a Royal request given to the Hero's party to journey to the village and to exterminate the demons. It has been noted that they are under suspicion that they could be working as a military base for demons. The possibility of getting a head start on taking over human owned land. Javier, Maya, and Gile gear up. They are met up front with the general of the Royal Guards. They have a group of guards with them. They head out towards the village. Two days later they arrived at the village's entryway.

"Alright men!" the General looks at Maya, "and women. We are about to enter the enemy line. Demons are known to be crafty. Take no prisoners and show no mercy!" the General says.

The crowd yells "Right!"

"Any words from our Hero?" the General asked.

Javier steps up.

"We're not here to start a war! We are here to finish it! If they attack us, we attack them! We are proud! We are strong! We will fight!" Javier yells.

The soldiers cheer. The soldiers begin piling in the entry of the village. The general signal them to stop. A demon approaches the front gate to meet with the army.

"Hello, we do not look for trouble," the demon said.

"You are on human property. We do not welcome your kind here. If you wish to take refugees, do it where your kind is welcomed!" The general said.

Javier didn't like how that sounded.

"Please, allow us to stay until the war..." the demon was cut off again.

"Denied! You demons are the reason we're going to war! You have exactly ten seconds to leave this village, or suffer the consequences," the General said.

"We beg for your mercy! Can't we reach a deal of some sort?" The demon asked.

"Here's the deal! Time's up! Fire the arrows," the general yelled.

Archers and Fire magic mages aimed and fired into the village.

"Charge!" the General yelled.

The men begin filling the village.

Lives are being taken on the demon side.

The Hero party runs towards the back of the village and into a house.

Three demons cower in the corner of their home. The two females are covered by a male demon standing in front of them.

"Please, we'll do anything. Don't hurt my family!" the demon pleaded.

Javier stands there shocked about the reaction. They aren't fighting back and pleading for life. Maya runs up to him.

"Javi, what's wrong?" Maya asked.

She looks in the house and sees the demons. Javier puts his weapons away and puts his hands up.

"Javi, what are you doing?" Maya asks.

"Trust me on this," Javier said.

He puts his hands up. He slowly walks towards the family.

He is three feet away from the family.

"Please," The male demon begs in sorrow.

Javier turns away from them, facing Maya.

"I thought so. Look closely, Maya. They aren't fighting back. They aren't looking to fight. They want a safe place away from the war," Javier said.

Maya looks outside and sees how one-sided the fight seems. Gile runs to Maya and Javier.

"What are you guys doing?" Gile says.

"I don't think we should continue," Javier said.

"Of course you'd say that. Now that you're part demon and suddenly..." Gile says.

"Look at them! My back is completely exposed to them. My hands are empty. They are fearing for their lives," Javier said.

"They're demons, they ruined our lives. They're a threat to the human race," Gile said.

Javier steps aside.

"You know what. Go ahead. Look them dead in their eyes and kill them," Javier said.

Gile walked up to them.

The male demon stood before the other two, shaking.

Gile lifts his axe. He swings down and hits only the floor.

"God damn it!" Gile said.

"This village isn't a secret base. It's a secret camp away from the Demon Kingdom," Javier said.

"So what do you plan to do?" Maya asked.

"We're stopping this massacre. Maya took these folks to the opposite side from where we came in. Gile, start collecting demons and take them where Maya is taking them. I'm going to try to stop the guards," Javier said.

"Javi, you better be right about this," Gile said.

"Gile, I'm putting my trust in you to help. I'm asking at this moment to do the same," Javier said.

Maya leads the demons out the end of the village. Gile starts escorting demons to the same area.

The general sees this from a distance.

"What are they doing?" the General asks.

Javier uses magic to project his voice across the village.

"Stop!" Javier yells.

Everyone stops and looks around for the one speaking.

"Notice how nobody on our side is even injured? This isn't a battle, it's an ambush. This village was abandoned a long time ago. Show me one demon that fought before you decided to attack. How many pleaded for their life before you went ahead and attacked them? I'm telling you as the Hero, retreat," Javier said.

The General does not like hearing him say this.

"We were here on King's orders," a soldier said.

"And you're going back on Hero's orders," Javier said.

Javier walks towards the center of the village.

"I'm telling you to stop, unless you have something to say to me personally. I'm right here. Do you think you can beat the Demon Lord without a Hero? I'll gladly leave it to you if you are against what I'm saying," Javier said.

The men slowly stop attacking.

"Go ahead and go home. If you wish to be helpful, then please line up in front of me. If you have too much human pride and don't agree with me, feel free to attack me at any time. I dare you!" Javier threatens.

Most of the soldiers exit the village. Javier opens a portal to the Royal Capital for them. A handful of healers and soldiers line up.

"Healers, I need you to go to the end of the village and start treating the demons. The rest of you, help carry the injured to the healers and search the buildings for anyone they have yet helped. We're handling things on my orders now," Javier said.

Javier walks towards the injured. He casts heal on his gun. Gile is standing on the side. Javier approaches him. He holds out his gun to Gile.

"Are you looking to help?" Javier asked.

Gile hesitated but eventually took the gun and started healing the demons.

A female demon ran up to Javier, "Please, you have to help me."

"Stay here until the soldiers leave," Javier said.

"Please, my son is still in our home that's on fire."

"Which house?" Javier asked.

The demon pointed at her home, Javier sighs.

"Stay here, I'll go get him," Javier said, running towards the house.

"His name is Rin," the demon said.

Javier gets to the front of the house. The General is standing in front of the doorway.

"What are you doing? The General said.

"There's a kid in that burning building. I'm trying to get him out. Get out of my way," Javier said.

"Demons are our enemy. A friend of Demons is an enemy of mine. I don't believe someone like you is our Hero if you won't fight for the greater good," the General said.

"We're not the good guys here in this situation. Now get out of my way or I'll force you out of my way," Javier said.

"You think you'll get away with putting your hands on a high-ranking soldier, especially the General," the General said.

"Let's find out," Javier said as he punched the General in the face, launching him yards away.

"That was me holding back. Don't make me go all out next time," Javier said.

Javier enters the burning building.

"Rin! Rin! Are you here?" Javier yelled.

"Help!" Javier heard muffled.

Javier busts through a door and sees the kid. Javier jumps towards the kid. The ceiling began caving in. The whole building went crashing down. It was quiet. The General smiled. The rubble started moving. Javier used earth magic to shield them and to move the rubble aside. He carries the boy to his mother. The mother hugs her son tight.

"Oh thank you! Thank you! Thank you!" The demon said.

"Keep an eye on your kid more," Javier said.

The demon nods.

All the surviving demons were treated and had the number of executed demons brought down. The Hero party and remaining soldiers were on their way back to the Royal Capital. They teleported to the Royal Capital entry. They were surprised by the guards.

"Hands behind your back Hero," a guard said.

"For what?" Javier said.

"You're under arrest for the suspicion of working with the Demon Kingdom," the guard said.

"What?" Maya questioned.

"Maya don't. I'll be fine," Javier said.

Javier was stripped of his weapons and poncho. They didn't notice the ring.

CHAPTER 21:
The Hero's Trial

(Part 1)

Javier has been arrested for the suspicion of working with the Demon Kingdom. Javier has been in a cell for a week now. Maya has visited him every day. Gile has visited him once. The Royal Capital has sent out Royal requests for the awaited trial. The trial took place days after the requests were sent out. Anyone who had enough contact with Javier would be taking the stand. The time for the trial began. Javier is standing with his hand tightly chained to the ground by powerful earth magic. A lot of people were talking and shocked that the Hero was on trial.

"Order! Order! Order! The trial is now taking place in the case of Javier Rios. A.K.A. The Hero. Under the suspicion that you're working with the Demon Kingdom, how do you plead?" The judge asked.

"Not guilty," Javier said.

"We will now bring in our first witness," The judge said.

The General took the stand.

"General Nick, it seems you had the most recent interaction with the Hero."

"That is correct, your honor," Nick said.

"Would you care to explain the situation?"

"We were sent on Orders from the King to make way to an abandoned city rumored to be demon headquarters. There were demons in that village, Human property. They were claiming to be refugees but had no documentation or authorization. We are trained to protect our country so we took a course of action and began trying to run the demons out of the village."

"That's not true!" Javier said.

"Silence! Continue General," the judge said.

"The Hero stepped in and started defending the demons. He manipulated soldiers into stopping our attack and helping the demons. I figured I was the last hope to talk some sense into him and he assaulted me," Nick said.

"Hero, did you defend the demons?" the judge asked.

"Yes, but..." Javier was cut off.

"We only need a Yes or No answer Hero."

"Yes," Javier answered.

"Did you have other soldiers help the demons?"

"Yes."

"Did General Nick try to stop you and you assaulted him?"

Javier sighs, "Yes."

The entire crowd gasps.

"We now bring the next witness."

Elly took the stand.

"Ms. Frey, I understand you were Javier's receptionist. Has Javier done anything that would insinuate trouble for the greater good?" The judge asked.

"No," Elly said.

"No further questions."

Maya took the stand.

"Ms. Lynn, after the departed party, the Hero's arrest, and rumors spreading; You've been by the Hero's side the entire time. Would you hide anything to protect your beloved partner?"

"Beloved partner? We're friends and party members," Maya said.

"Is that so? We do have a witness who saw you and the hero did take part in intimate activities," The judge said.

An employee from the "Dragon Hot Spring" was brought to the stand.

"Mr. Smith, would you kindly explain what it is you saw?"

"Well I was cleaning the changing rooms and noticed there were two people in the mixed bath. I didn't want to rush or make them get out so I continued cleaning. I look over and they are very close. Then I saw them make suggestive looks and they kissed," the employee said.

"Okay wait, that was a long time ago and that meant nothing. That doesn't prove Javier of being guilty of anything," Maya said.

"Perhaps not, but it does abstain you from taking the stand."

"This is rigged," Javier thought.

Gile was next to take the stand.

"Mr. Rockman, you were there at the village. Have you noticed that Javier wasn't assisting the guards?" the judge asked.

Gile hesitated,"Yes."

"So it further proves that Javier had no intention to assist the human race and to help the demon race."

"No, I don't believe so," Gile said.

"Would you elaborate?" the judge asked.

"Javier came on the mission and was ready to fight the demons. In Javier's view, it was a massacre. The demons were not fighting back and were not looking to harm us. Javier noticed it and put a stop to it. He believed he was doing the right thing, and I support that he is doing the right thing," Gile said.

"No further questions. We will now take a 30-minute recess and will pick the case back up at noon," The judge said.

The judge was seen walking with Harry and the King. The three of them entered a room together.

"You're not keeping your end of the deal," Harry said to the judge.

"I'm only asking questions that lead to showing the Hero's guilt. I have to make it look fair," the judge said.

"Remember that my word is absolute, if you don't convince everyone that the peasant is guilty, I will lock up you and your family. I'm sure your daughter wouldn't like prison very much," the King said.

"I understand," the judge said.

"I hope you do. That Hero has disrespected royals and their

authority for the last time. His attitude is unwelcomed to the Kingdom and we will make sure he never gets the respect of the people again," Harry said.

Elly, Maya, Gile, and Lily visit Javier's cell.

"This trial is rigged," Javier said.

"I agree," Maya said.

"It's obvious. The judge seemed to struggle when I was clearing you of good nature," Gile said.

"Thanks Gile, I appreciate that," Javier said.

"Of course, what are friends for?" Gile said.

Javier grins slightly.

"Don't get me wrong, I still haven't 100% forgiven you but I understand where you're coming from and I will make sure that you don't get a bad representation of your name," Gile said.

"Neither will I," Leo said walking towards Javier's cell.

"Leo?" Javier asked, shocked.

"Been a while disgraceful Hero," Leo said and smirked.

"How are you?" Javier asked.

"Well, I realized that when I wanted my family to forgive me, it's more that I couldn't forgive myself. It made me realize that I didn't see it from your point of view and didn't give you much of a chance to explain. It was bottled emotions that I let out on you and blamed you for all my trouble, so I'm sorry for that," Leo said.

"It's cool. I wanted an upper hand against the Demon Lord so that's why I did it but by how things are looking, I'm not sure if I can make it through this trial. The judge is trying to find the smallest piece to exploit whatever it is that says that I'm working undercover for the Demon Kingdom. Are they forgetting that I'm the Hero? There is a war that's going to happen very soon and it doesn't seem like they are getting prepared for it," Javier said, annoyed.

"That's exactly what you're going to say when you take the stand. In the end, let them know that the trial feels rigged and that the Demon Lord is coming whether they are ready or not," Leo said.

Javier nods.

"Javi, is everything going to be okay?" Lily asked.

"I don't know Lily, but don't worry. I'll figure it out," Javier said to Lily.

"Well, as long as we stick together, we can still figure a way out of this," Elly said.

"I sure hope so," Javier said.

CHAPTER 22:
THE HERO'S TRIAL

(Part 2)

The trial is now back in session. Things are looking good in the king's favor. People that Javier helped or saved took the stand. One abstain after another. The judge is getting frustrated because no one is giving him enough to exploit other than the General. Things were looking like they were coming to a close until Harry pulled the ace up his sleeve.

"We will now have Doctor Fern on the stand," the judge said.

Javier feels a little uneasy. He doesn't exactly trust Fern. Fern can go either way in this situation.

"Mr. Fern, there is speculation that the Hero has a connection with demons. Do you know anything about that? Many have spotted Javier visits your shop quite often," the judge said.

Fern didn't expect the judge to ask that as the first question and worded it differently than anyone else.

"Mr. Fern it has come to my attention that you have enough charges to be put away for life and anything you worked towards can be lost. If you comply, all the charges will be dropped and responsibility with your aid will be overlooked," the judge said.

Fern is being put in the corner. Fern is hesitating too much. He gave Javier a look that said he apologized, but he was trying to save his skin.

"That damn doc," Javier thought.

"Yes, Javier is connected to a demon," Fern says.

The crowd gasps. Things are starting to fall into place for the King.

"Mr. Fern, can you elaborate?" the judge asks.

Fern hesitates.

"Mr. Fern you're under oath, speak clearly and truthfully," the Judge said.

Fern cracks "Javier made a deal with a demon and now has demon abilities," Fern said.

Javier glares at Fern.

"Is this demon among us?" the judge asked.

Fern looked at the party and then Javier.

The judge noticed that.

"Please have the party lined up please," the judge says.

The party is lined up.

"Elly is clear, Leo is clear, Gile is clear Maya is clear, Li," the judge read.

"I must be reading this wrong but Lily's file doesn't seem to add up. Her last name is Rios but she looks nothing like the Hero. The Hero is from another world and has been here for nearly 5 months, meaning there is no blood relation. You also don't have adoption papers so it's as if Lily doesn't exist," the judge said.

Everyone but Lily is being moved off the stand. A man comes up next to Lily.

"This man's magic set consists of special magic that can negate magic," the judge said.

There seems to be magic flowing around her head.

"Wait, I'll confess! Don't do it!" Javier said.

"I'm sorry, Mr. Rios, it's a little too late for that. Do it," the judge said.

The man negates the light magic used on Lily. Lily's white hair and crimson eyes are clear as day to everyone.

Gasps and screams are echoing across the audience.

"Ladies and gentlemen, a demon has been a part of the Hero's party and the Hero has been hiding her," the judge said.

The look on Javier, and the party's faces was as if they saw the most important person to them was murdered in cold blood.

"Fern I'll kill you!" Javier roared.

"I'm afraid that is not all, demons are not allowed within the Kingdom so we must execute the demon and Javier has been found guilty!" the judge said, as he taps the desk with his gavel.

"No!" Elly screamed.

"You can't do that!" Gile yelled.

"Javi!" Lily screamed

"Don't you touch her!" Javier yelled.

Javier slides his thumb on his ring and has been set to Level 3.

An executioner has a hand on Lily and another on a slashing weapon.

"No!" Javier yells in a demonic voice.

The entire place went silent.

They see Javier's hair is half black and half white, his left pupil turned red but the white of his left eye turned black, his left claw came out, and he grew his left wing out. Javier broke the chains with ease and circled Lily to get everyone to back away from her.

"Don't you touch her!" Javier said.

"Checkmate Hero," the King said.

The whole audience screamed and ran out of the courtroom.

Javier grabbed Lily and ran away with her. He rushed to the storage room and grabbed his weapons. The party followed Javier. Javier opened a portal and it closed when he and the party jumped through. They appeared in Elly's old town guild. Everyone in that guild saw Javier and chaos broke out.

"Javi, somewhere where this isn't people, and turn your ring off!" Maya said.

Javier turned down his level. They appeared where Javier first showed up in the new world.

"Wait, why did you guys come with me?" Javier asked.

"We're just as guilty as you now," Leo said.

"This situation is dreadful," Gile said.

"Is there anywhere we can go?" Maya asked.

"I think I know of one place," Javier said.

Javier opened up a portal and the group walked in.

They appeared at the entry of "Nomans Village."

The demons were shocked to see the Hero again. They welcomed him with open arms though.

"Hero, what are you doing here?" a demon asked.

"Well we're kind of on the run now. This is Lily. We were hiding that she was a demon and well that is no longer a secret," Javier said.

The one in charge of the village walked up.

"You helped us when we were at our weakest point and treated our wounds. We will gladly take you in. We've been thinking of expanding and learning illusion magic so they can't find this town," the leader said.

"We greatly appreciate it," Elly said.

Leo is very standoffish.

"What the hell is going on? Leo asked.

"Oh, right. When you left we had a quest to come to this village to fight the demons, but Javier of course did his usual thing and stopped the royal guards from doing too much damage," Gile said.

"No need to worry Leo, they aren't bad demons. They're quite nice," Maya said.

"Hero, this is perfect. There is a Demon who helps us out every once in a while. We talked about you and said she wanted to meet you and thank you personally," a demon said.

"Oh uh, sure," Javier said.

They lead Javier to a building where they have dinner and standing there is someone he never thought he would see in this situation.

"Oh, my God," Javier said.

Nino stood there while she was serving the demon's food and she just froze when she made eye contact with Javier.

"Javi, do you know who that is?" Elly asked.

"Um, nope, never seen her in my life," Javier said dismissively.

"Perverted Hero," Nino said while gritting her teeth.

"Perverted Hero?" both Maya and Elly asked.

A demon walked in with another pot of food.

"Alright General, I finished the next pot of Perverted Hero!" said Saki.

"Alright I don't know what the hell is going on," Leo said.

CHAPTER 23:
Reunion

"Perverted Hero!" Saki said.

"She's here too?" Javier asked.

Saki lays down the pot and gets in Javier's face.

"You got a lot of nerve to show your face here!" Saki said.

"You're one to talk, why are you even here?" Javier said back.

"This village of demons needs help and I care about them!" Saki said.

"Funny you say that because I helped this village from an attack by royal guards!" Javier said.

"Okay I think we should calm down," Elly said.

"I'm not sure, Nino over there is staring daggers at me. I knew she missed me," Javier said sarcastically.

Nino puts down the ladle, takes off her apron and asks Javier to come outside.

Javier follows.

"Do they have bad blood or something?" Gile asked.

"The perverted hero." Saki said.

Nino and Javier are two feet apart. Nino breathed deeply and then lunged at Javier. Javier jumped back to evade Nino.

"You'll pay for what you did to me, you scumbag Hero," Nino said.

"I told you it was an accident! You think I wanted to do that?" Javier asked.

Nino is swinging non stop at Javier while Javier keeps dodging.

"You think you can grab my breast and get away with it?" Nino yelled.

"As I keep trying to say, you're the one who lunged at me and that's just how we landed," Javier said as he tripped back the exact moment Nino lunged so she landed on top of him.

Nino and Javier landed in the same position again but this time on the floor.

Nino is embarrassed and Javier is annoyed.

"Get off of me!" Javier said and pushed Nino off.

Javier's group and Saki came running out.

"General, are you okay?" Saki asked.

"He did it again!" Nino said.

"Huh?" Saki asked.

"Huh?" Elly asked.

"Huh?" Maya asked.

"I didn't do it on purpose! You fell on top of me!" Javier said.

"Everybody needs to stop fighting!" Lily said.

"Lily, I think you should let the adults handle it," Javier said.

Nino gets up and walks towards Lily.

"Lily?" Nino asked.

Lily looked at Nino confused.

"It's me, Nino," Nino said.

Lily paused for a second.

Lily then ran up to Nino and hugged her.

"Nino!" Lily yelled.

"You two know each other?" Javier asked.

"I took care of her when she was even younger. So how do YOU know her?" Nino asked.

"We were watching after her when we rescued her from slave traders," Javier said.

Nino sighed. There was silence for a few moments.

"I still hate your guts but for now, let's call a truce," Nino said.

"I refuse! I don't like this perverted Hero!" Saki said.

"Saki..." Nino said.

Saki sucked her teeth.

"Sure, truce," Javier said but still had his guard up.

They all went back to the dining hall. They ate dinner and talked about what happened and how The Hero's party got there.

"I understand. Thank you for looking after Lily. You don't have to worry about her anymore," Nino said.

"What the hell are you talking about?" Javier said.

"I thought Lily was gone forever, but now that I reunited with her, she'll be staying with me," Nino explained.

"Not a chance in hell!" Javier said.

"Stop!" Lily yelled.

The entire table calmed down.

Everyone is turning in for the night. Lily is staying with Elly for the night.

Javier walks to Nino's room. He knocks on her door frame. Nino turned round and backed up against the wall when she saw Javier.

"Relax, I'm not here to start a problem. I wanted to talk to you," Javier said.

"What for?" Nino questioned.

"I want to talk about the future and what I'm planning to do," Javier explained.

"Why would I care what you do?" Nino asked.

"Well... I see that we both have a similar interest and possibly end goal. I think if you hear me out we can maybe work something out?" Javier asked.

"Absolutely not," Nino said.

"You didn't even give me a chance to explain myself," Javier said.

"Not interested. Now get out of my room," Nino said.

She kicks Javier out of her room. Javier decides to go back to his room but runs into Saki.

"Pervert Hero?" Saki asked.

"Can you just call me Javier?" Javier asked, annoyed.

"What were you doing in the General's room?" Saki asked out of suspicion.

"Nothing really. I tried talking to her but she didn't want to give me a chance," Javier said.

"What did you want to talk about?" Saki asked.

"Nothing, don't worry about it. Sorry I bothered you," Javier said.

Saki grabs Javier's hand. Javier looks back at her in confusion.

"What are you doing?" Javier asked.

"I'm worried about the General," Saki said.

"What's wrong with Nino?" Javier asked.

"Follow me," Saki said.

Javier decided to follow Saki. They enter Saki's room. Saki closes the door.

"The Demon Lord removed both me and Nino from power," Saki said.

"Okay? Why?" Javier asked.

"When we explained our interaction we had with you and deemed us unsuitable for his plans. We were practically kicked out of the Kingdom's forces," Saki said.

"That's harsh," Javier asked.

"Nino is thinking about starting a revolution. She disagrees with how the Kingdom is being run but doesn't have enough power on her own to take on the Demon Lord," Saki said.

"So you want me to help her?" Javier asked.

"Yes," Saki says.

"I see. No."

"Huh?"

"I doubt that it would work. She doesn't even like me. Working with her isn't going to be easy," Javier said.

"I wouldn't ask you unless I had to. Of course I'll help her, but that isn't enough. Most citizens are scared of the demon

Lord because of his ruthless punishment if anyone steps out of line. And I don't just mean you. We need all of you. Nino is too stubborn to admit it but we really could use your help," Saki said.

Javier sat there for a second.

"I don't think the rest of my group would agree to something that crazy," Javier said.

"Could you please talk to them?" Saki asked.

"So let me get this straight. You want me to convince my crew, who hate when I do stupid things to join a demon who doesn't like me, to start a revolution in the Demon Kingdom along with other demons?" Javier asked.

"Please, I'll call you Javier if you do," Saki asked.

"I don't care what you call me that much," Javier said.

They sit there quietly for a few moments. Javier sees Saki's face and can tell she is genuine. Javier sucks his teeth.

"Fine, I'll see what I can do, but I won't promise anything," Javier said.

"Really?" Saki asked.

"Well defeating the Demon Lord is my goal anyway, having a few strong demons on my side would give me more confidence. Anyways, I'm turning in for the night. We'll talk later," Javier said.

Saki leaned forward and kissed Javier on the cheek. Javier has no idea how to react to that and walks out. He closes the door and Nino walks out of the closet.

"Good work Saki," Nino said.

"You could've asked him yourself," Saki said.

"Absolutely not, I'd rather fail than personally ask that perverted hero for his help. Why did you kiss him though?" Nino asked.

"Let's not worry about that. Now we need to focus on the next phase in our plan. Are you sure this is the best route to take?" Saki asked.

"There aren't many options and the war will be here. I want to end this with as little bloodshed as possible," Nino explains.

"Can we really trust the Hero and his group?" Saki concerns.

There was a slight pause.

"I'm not so sure but I have faith since we have the same goal in mind," Nino says.

Javier was standing outside the door hearing the conversation. Javier sighs out of frustration.

"This is going to be one hell of a mission. That damn goddess," Javier thought

To be continued...

www.ingramcontent.com/pod-product-compliance
Lightning Source LLC
LaVergne TN
LVHW090610110826
845146LV00001B/327

* 9 7 9 8 2 3 4 0 1 4 6 0 3 *